Bridging the Tides

Amanda Zieba

To Katie —

"And above all, watch with glittering eyes the world around you, because the greatest treasures are always hidden in the most unlikely places. Those who do not believe in magic will never find it."

— Roald Dahl

Happy Reading!

♡,
Amanda Zieba

Published by Amanda Zieba
Copyright May 2015

ISBN: 978-1511708449
Type Sets: Bookman Antiqua, Free Style Script, Arial Narrow

Dedication

This book is dedicated to the women in my family who are doers... degree earners, world travelers, business starters, fixers, mountain climbers, prayer-sayers, cheerleaders, family-raisers and dream chasers. Thank you for showing me that no matter what we choose to do in life, it is possible.

Bridging the Tides

One bridge leads to a happy ending,
Another to darkest dispair.
Which begs your mind to question,
What is right and what is fair?

One bridge crosses calm waters
Ane one traverses choppy seas.
A bridge to friend ship or betrayal
Which choice will it be?

The tides are coming in now,
Let your path be your voice.
Whose cause do you favor?
Which bridge will be your choice?

It has been a week...

since Flynn returned to the ARK to help the crew battle the remants of an experiment gone wrong and search for their missing parents and friend Carl. Long gone are her days of sunshine and shopping. Here to stay are days and nights of danger. But she isn't in the fight alone.

Professor Solomon Sorenson, the brilliant man who built the ARK, has journeyed to the ocean floor with her to add his brain power to the team of teen scientists, one little brother, and a growing army of animal allies. Still on the surface, Nora and Simon, a duo of long distance help, await their orders.

Above the water and below they are working to reverse the catastrophic side effects of PE-328.

Chapter 1
ARK

"Nothing astonishes men so much as common sense and plain dealing." – Ralph Waldo Emerson

Blood in the water. Never a good sign.

It hung there, suspended and twisting in the slow current outside the observation deck window. The blood was there yesterday and the day before, the same as it was today. Caspian assured Flynn it would be there tomorrow and the day after that. But Flynn still couldn't get used to it, couldn't wrap her head around it.

If there hadn't been blood, Flynn's mind might have wandered to the surface. To Nora. To the sun. To Alex. To the life she was forced to leave. If there hadn't been blood she might have been thinking about the change she saw in her older brother, and the naturally pretty face who seemed to fit in down here better than Flynn ever had. If there hadn't been blood, Flynn would have been worrying about her missing parents.

But there was blood. A lot of it.

At first the grotesque intimidation tactics had gone unnoticed. The drapes covering their window to the world had shielded the ARK crew from Adonis' brutality. At the command of the ruthless dolphin, the view from the window showed a landscape littered with animal remains. Some of them weren't quite dead yet, and as their hearts beat their last, blood pumped from their slashed bodies into the water.

Blood in the water.

Caspian had told Flynn about the several times daily deliveries shortly after she arrived down in the ARK. Caspian had been meeting with 'Cuda the first time he saw the deadly display. 'Cuda informed him it had been happening regularly for days. Before long, they could depend on the administrations to arrive like clockwork.

Blood in the water.

"Earth to Flynn?"

"Ah, sorry," Flynn said, dragging her gaze from the blood and back to the breakfast meeting.

They were discussing their plan of action. They had been discussing it to death – literally, the plan was dead. There was no plan. The discussion now revolved around which of their problems was the top priority and therefore deserving of their full attention.

Yet, Flynn couldn't blame them. They were scientists. They lived their lives in theory. It wasn't surprising that when modern society took decades to fund their theories, they weren't used to jumping into a plan of action without fully and totally thinking it through. Before Flynn had spent three (glorious!) months living on the surface, she found these types of circling conversations highly annoying. Now, she found them positively maddening.

"To continue discussion on the communication system is pointless. We have already decided to handle this problem in house," Caspian voiced, not for the first time, drawing an exaggerated sigh from Anton, who sat with his square jaw clenched shut tightly.

"I'd say it has escalated past the status of "problem"," Pac interjected oblivious to the tension in the room.

"Point taken Pac, but nevertheless, cross communications off the list," Professor Bebee instructed.

Sonora, acting as secretary, drew a line through the word *communication* on the white board that had been stuck to the front of the industrial-sized fridge.

"So that leaves us with: creating an antidote for PE-328, repairing the ARK, gathering intelligence reports from allied sources, finding our parents and replenishing supplies."

"Well what is available at the Outlier Station? Maybe that will solve our supply problem," Flynn asked. When met with silence she continued. "I'm sure if we checked the Outlier inventory reports we'd be able to at least have an estimate of what supplies would be available to us. There's gotta be something helpful out there."

"When we saw all communication ties were cut," Caspian began slowly "we just crossed the Outlier Station off our list entirely. We never even considered the other possibilities it held."

"Like food," Luke added, fueling the conversation forward.

"Or full oxygen tanks," Stillman suggested.

"Or ingredients for a PE-328 antidote," Anton shouted out, taking the opportunity to push his agenda.

"Or how about our parents?" Flynn surprised even herself with the level of calm in her voice. But the calm vanished instantly, giving way to a maelstrom of chaos.

"Oh my gosh," Nina gasped.

"Why didn't we…" Sonora started.

"Holy sea silt," Pac swore.

"Do you think they are really there?!?" Noah asked.

"Maybe Carl is there too! He never came back from that disaster of a mission to the kep forest and no has seen a sign of him since!" Anton shouted.

Ten minutes after Professor Bebee gave up trying to silence them, it took Professor Sorenson another ten minutes to wrangle the wild emotions into order.

"Enough!" he bellowed. When they had finally quieted he said again in a tired voice, "Enough. Clearly Flynn's fresh perspective on the situation-"

"Dude, way past situation," said Pac.

"-has been immensely helpful, unlike some unproductive comments," Professor Sorenson continued, shooting Pac a warning look. "Now, let's get to work on a plan for travel to the Outlier Station and retrieval of whatever,"

"Or whomever," said a voice identifiable to all, despite the fact it was ducking under the table to avoid certain injury from an angry looking mustached face.

"Whatever or whoever might be there," Professor Sorenson spit out measuredly.

"I hate to be a tsunami of despair, but I'm not sure leaving undetected is a possible option."

Flynn pointed to the observation deck window where Adonis' henchmen were delivering a fresh supply of carcasses. Once again the usually picturesque view was tainted by blood in the water.

Chapter 2
Surface

"If you don't design your own life, chances are you'll fall into someone else's plan. And guess what they have planned for you? Not much." – Jim Rohn

Nora sat at the kitchen island, spooning bites of cereal in her mouth. Her morning daze was slowly wearing off, bite by generic bite. As the fog in her brain lifted, she became increasingly aware of her surroundings. Her parents floating around the island, pouring coffee, trading sections of the newspaper, making their plans for Saturday. Luke, waiting at her feet, hoping for some table scraps, his collar and tags jangling slightly as she rubbed him with her bare foot. The TV, tuned to a local station, was attempting to educate them on the daily news.

"I know it sounds crazy, but I tell you, it's true!" a gravelly voice harangued.

Nora knew that voice. It wedged itself down under her mental fog and forced it to clear.

"We hadn't caught anything in weeks. Nuttin'. And tha's rare. Usually October is a good month for fishermen in Florida. But we didn't catch a minnow. It was that way through almost all of November and then all of a sudden, BAM!" he shouted, his voice rising with the excitement of his story. "BAM! That one day, our nets were just full of everything! Not just our normal haul either. We caught mackerel, mahi, grouper, angel fish, dolphins... everything!"

"I know him!" Nora screeched, sliding her stool away from the counter. She squished Luke's tail in the process, and set him to howling and turning circles in the kitchen.

"Shut up Luke!" Nora shouted and grabbed the remote

to turn up the volume.

"Goodness Nora, is that necessary?" Mrs. Nelson asked, grabbing Luke's collar, trying to calm him down.

"Shh!" hissed Nora, completely absorbed in the newscast.

"Nora! Don't speak to your mother that way!" her father scolded.

"Ugh, forget it!" Nora huffed seeing that, due to the kitchen chaos, she had missed the rest of Roy's segment. Pausing only to deposit her cereal bowl in the sink, she ran up the stairs two at a time. Upon entering her room she grabbed her laptop and raced to BayCity7News.com. In a few clicks she had the full story and more.

Her eyes raced across the screen, reading the dictated quotes of the story. Another click brought her to the archived episode of the news and she watched again as the salty captain told his story. Nora could still close her eyes and see Roy in the dingy bait shop, laughing as he sold Flynn and her buckets full of sinkers and lures. She never would have imagined him newsworthy in any light, but here he was, in the morning spotlight slot, all of Bay City listening to him describe his crazy catch.

But Captain Roy wasn't the only one making the newsreel this morning. While browsing the site Nora found a small story on a missing person's report. Apparently the university, not to mention Mrs. Sorenson, had noticed the disappearance of a certain celebrated professor and a full scale search was about to be launched.

A knock on the door drew Nora's attention away from her computer screen. Her dad was standing half in, half out of her doorway, a stern look on his face.

"Can we talk?" he asked. Nora ushered with her hand and he took a seat on the end of her bed. "I know you are upset Flynn has left. It was a really big bummer that she got called down for that important experiment. But until Nina returns at the end of the school year, you are going to have to deal with being an only child and all of the attention that comes with it. Lately your attitude has gone beyond normal moody teenage mode and it has to stop. Your mother and I are asking you, to figure it out, and if you can't, you're going to find yourself grounded pretty fast."

Figure it out?!? Figure it out. I'm trying to. If only I knew what was going on down there right now.

"So can you?"

I don't know.

"That wasn't a rhetorical question Nora." Nora nodded, blinking back tears.

"I'm going for a run before work," she said, standing suddenly, reaching for her dresser to find the appropriate attire, hoping her father would get the hint and leave.

"Alright, good idea. Burn off some of that stress in a positive way," he said, moving toward the door. "Remember what we talked about." Again Nora nodded and after he walked out she collapsed back on her bed, socks and sports bra in hand.

Figure it out. Get it together. Get it done. Get... she tried to pep talk herself into a solution. But none came.

Chapter 3
Underwater Cave

"So come out of your cave walking on your hands, and see the world hanging upside down. You can understand dependence when you know the maker's land." – The Cave, Mumford and Sons

Dark and dangerous deeds should be done in dark and dangerous places. It seemed fitting that Adonis should choose to make his headquarters in the depths of a sea cave. A wide open space with protected access to the oxygen the dolphins needed to survive made this location positively perfect. Currently his pod was hiding out in the cubbyhole caves spread out through the labyrinth that stretched behind and beyond the main cave. Even though Adonis was the only dolphin in the gigantic cavern, he was not alone.

He looked over the gathered creatures and was pleased by the turnout. Several representatives from local schools, herds and pods surrounded him in the limestone cavern. King mackerel, tuna, angelfish, threadfin, mahi and swordfish … the large and the small, the colorful and the strong, the dangerous and unsuspecting… all here to show their loyalty and join his side of the war. He named each creature a warrior and selected a member of each kind to bear the title commander. He was now instructing them on the plan of action. Each phase was to render the humans both fearful and helpless.

"I am not just some maniac who swims here before you, raging about the humans. I come before you with a plan and the power to accomplish it. The world has known too much destruction at the hands of the land-walkers. They must be stopped. Who will rise with me to put these humans in their place?"

A chorus of rowdy cheers echoed through the cave. The sound traveled back to the far reaches of the labyrinth off the main great room and bounced back at them.

"The goal is to scare them into doing nothing. We will paralyze them with fear. And while they are doing nothing, we will get to work," Adonis continued

"What exactly is that work?" asked Commander Hale. Although he was a fraction of the size of the fish that surrounded him, his fearless voice filled the flooded cavern.

Annoyed at being questioned Adonis fixed a beady black eye on the angelfish. "Quite bold for one so small," he began. "It is not for you to know yet."

"Forgive me sir. It is just that I am so thirsty for revenge. These humans steal our young and trap them in bowls and tanks. I am anxious to put their evil ways to an end."

Appeased, Adonis relaxed his wrath toward the fish and corrected him. "Not an end to their ways, Commander Hale. An end to them. An end to the humans' existence."

The meeting continued without further interruptions. Tasks were delegated, duties carried out, and new plans made. When the warriors and commanders were dismissed and dispersed Adonis remained in the cave.

"Make them fearful. Make them helpless," he repeated as he swam alone in the cave, willing them to be true.

Chapter 4
ARK

"I hadn't appreciated <u>before</u> when I'd been there. But now, <u>before</u> was where I wanted to be, <u>before</u> was where I wanted to live."
– from: One Came Home by Amy Timberlake

Flynn had hoped that keeping her hands busy would do the same for her mind. Computer troubleshooting used to be her ticket to escape. Fingers typing, mouse clicking, mind whirring – it was nearly impossible for anything else to crowd in. But with the communications and computer systems down, and a dismal outlook of their repair on the horizon, there was no such happy oblivion for Flynn today.

Ever since discovering the possible location of their parents, every waking hour was devoted to figuring out how to get to the Outlier Station safely. Safely being the key word.

She'd been back a week. A solid week of supply organizing and data collecting, plan formulating and data analyzing. Everything she hated about living in the ARK crashed down around her in perfectly calculated precision. One week. Seven days of hard work and they still hadn't made any real progress other than talking about a plan. But even that statement was a stretch. They had decided the target goal to form their plan around. Flynn supposed it was better than nothing, but a plan was not action. Action would drive away the worries buzzing her brain like the mosquitos in the Nelson's backyard. Action was the ticket to her sanity she decided, but action was nowhere in sight.

Instead she was monitoring the jellyfish. It was the opposite of action, which was dangerous. As Jett and his parental units floated aimlessly in Noah's once grand underwater playground, she was supposed to be looking for signs of human intelligence, other than speaking. Even though they were all in mortal danger, apparently (according to the professors and Caspian) the validity of their experiment-gone-wrong could not be compromised.

So she sat, next to Sonora, resident animal behavior expert, watching Jett avoid his parents as much as possible in an enclosed tank, which seemed pretty human-esque in Flynn's opinion.

"So it must have been really amazing, huh?" Sonora asked, eyes fixed on the tank.

"What? Oh, yeah," Flynn answered.

"Because you've been a complete Jellyfish-"

"Hey!" Jett piped up.

"Sorry Jett!" Sonora apologized and then finished, "Since you got back."

"It's like reverse culture shock, depression and buyer's remorse all rolled in one."

"No wonder you look so gills up," Jett commented as he glided past them.

"Hey, now it's my turn to be offended," Flynn shot back, but her heart wasn't in it enough to come out with her usual sass.

"Sorry," Jett said, making another lap around the tank.

"Forgiven," she called out as Jett swam away. When he reached the far side of the tank she added, "Plus the whole talking animal thing is still really weirding me out."

"Yeah, I suppose we've had more time to adjust to the idea. It almost seems strange when I think about the way things used to be. I mean, you might think I'm crazy, but hear me out."

"I'm all ears," Flynn said.

"I'm not," Jett chimed in gliding past them again, "but I'm listening."

"As someone in the zoology field, I hypothesize there would be benefits in being able to communicate with animals in a complex manner such as human speech. Just think of all that we could learn! And all the good we could do with that information." Sonora spoke passionately and Flynn admired her for it.

"You make some good points, but I think you're going to be fighting against the current when you bring this up with the others."

"I know," Sonora said sadly. "I just don't entirely want things to go back to the way things used to be."

Flynn's eyes brimmed with tears she couldn't hold back. "I do," she said softly as the tears fell and tracked down her sun kissed cheeks.

If things went back to the way they were before, her parents wouldn't be missing. Her brothers and crewmates wouldn't look like ghosts of their former selves – hollow eyed and pale. If things went back to the way they were before, Professor Bebee would still keep up her usually immaculate appearance, instead of covering her short grey locks with a patterned scarf. She would still wear her snappy suits and decorative broaches beneath her lab coat. She would lecture them about the wonders of the ocean instead of preparing them for imminent battle. If things went back to normal, Noah would laugh and play Obscoral all day. He wouldn't insist on permanently attaching himself to his big brother. He would sleep peacefully through the night.

The ARK was an empty shell of its former existence. It was too quiet. If things were like they had been before they would laugh at Pac's jokes and meals would be fun instead of functional. It was like they were all actors impersonating the people she once knew, trying to be themselves and failing miserably.

Herself included. No longer was she the spunky fashion obsessed girl dying for a new life. Flynn stared at her reflection in the tank glass, hating that her coveted tan cheeks marked her as a deserter and that her tears marked her as weak. She hated the view she saw, and the person she saw staring back. Basically, she just hated it all.

"We'll fix this," Flynn said to no one in particular. "I don't know how yet, but we will."

Chapter 5
Surface

"I am convinced that boredom is one of the greatest tortures. If I were to imagine Hell, it would be the place where you are continually bored." – Erich Fromm (from The Dogma of Christ)

Boredom. Sheer, utter and complete boredom. This was the definition of Nora's part time job. The endless nothingness was enough to drive her insane. Still, banking on a hefty soccer scholarship, Nora did not see the necessity of a job, but her parents said she shouldn't "rest on her laurels", whatever that meant, and made her get one anyway. Fall soccer was done and spring soccer lay a maddening four months away. She was in a purgatory period which, instead of running, scoring and living, she was selling smoothies.

So the Smoothie Shak it was. Given the little tiki hut's off-beach location, customers were few and far between. She could count on a few visits from the elderly occupants of the senior community center around the block, but that was about it. The annoyance for her job grew daily as she pulled on the obnoxiously lame company uniform (a Hawaiian print shirt). The name tag was the final straw that broke her threshold of tolerance. Above her name in neon orange letters it read: Smoothie Shak.

Everyone knows "shak" is really spelled "shack". So why leave out the C? Will this clever marketing trick really convince more people to buy a healthy fruit drink from the cute girl at the tiki hut? Feeling rebellious, or bored, she couldn't decipher which emotion was stronger, she grabbed a Sharpie and added the letter C to her name tag.

School would be starting up again in two days. While she was looking forward to the brain numbing classwork she hoped would take her mind off her currently long list of problems, she couldn't help but feel a twinge of sadness at going through it without Flynn. God she missed her.

Boredom led to sadness, followed by guilt. Thinking about Flynn brought back memories of the events below the surface and the battle raging below. Suddenly serving smoothies to senior citizens didn't seem so bad. Thinking about Flynn also reminded Nora that she was supposed to be working on a plan. As much as Nora loved a project, she was starting to realize that working on one solo was far less fun.

Alright Nora, focus. A plan. You need a plan. How can we control the animals below? Could we trap them? We would need a massive effort by on shore humans. And we would need to get the word out without issuing an all-points bulletin panic attack. We need... We need...

"Hello Nora, we need two Strawberry Shooter Smoothies please," greeted an elderly gentleman clad in a suspiciously similar Hawaiian shirt.

"Oh, hi Mr. Fields." Nora was drawn away from her daydreams and snapped into action. As she mixed the smoothie ingredients for Mr. Fields and his lady friend Mrs. DelRay, (whom insisted she call them Norman and Florence), Nora mixed her thoughts, trying to come up with the right recipe for a successful plan. She would have to talk to Alex. Aside from being in on the secret, he was the only one who truly understood the absolute urgency of it all.

Nora handed over the two smoothies, accepted the cash (including a one dollar tip!) from Mr. Fields and watched the couple shuffle back to the senior center. With her customers' needs met, Nora leaned back against the counter and stared out at the horizon. When the sun set three hours, two customers and zero realistic ideas later, she closed up shop and headed home.

Chapter 6
ARK

"Do what you can, with what you have, where you are."
– Teddy Roosevelt

It was hard for Flynn to watch them. Their eye contact, their romantic blushes, their supposedly inconspicuous hand holding. Their love in general, was so evident it was almost choking Flynn to have to swallow the fact that her scientifically sheltered, fashion backward, brains-over-brawn brother had found his *one* before she had.

Flynn wasn't stupid enough to believe she would really meet her *one* in her short time on the surface, but it was salt water to the wound to see that someone else had. She had only spared a few minutes to think about Alex since she had returned to the ARK. If she was honest with herself, she knew that losing Alex was minimal in comparison to losing Nora.

No, she had not lost Nora. She just couldn't be with her right now. Flynn had no idea how she would cope if she actually had lost her best friend, so she pushed those thoughts from her mind as soon as they surfaced. Besides, she would remind herself almost instantly, *you have bigger fish to fry right now. Literally.*

Flynn looked up at the magnetic whiteboard that continually served as their visual thinking space. At the top in big black letters it said: "Get to the Outlier Station" and underneath it was a list of supplies necessary to travel to there. Number one on the list: a mode of transportation. Taped up next to the whiteboard was a map with the ARK and Outlier Station clearly marked. Surrounding both buildings were post-it notes stuck to various locations where enemy scouts were thought to be located. Pac and Luke had been out doing a bit of spying. Enhancing their information with the reports Caspian was getting from 'Cuda, the sources combined were thought to be pretty accurate. Traveling the mere mile looked to be about as complicated as traversing a landmine-filled battlefield.

Well, it's missing about forty-seven bullet points worth of instructions, Flynn mused. *But at least it's a start. Maybe our parents really are there. Maybe once the rest of the adults get back they will have more information to share. Maybe, maybe... maybe...* Flynn finished her meager breakfast and stood to take her dishes to the sink, her mind drifting to their conversation at dinner last night.

"Don't forget they are masters of camouflage," Stillman had said. "So even if the way looks clear, chances are, it's not."

"What we need is a tank," Noah decided. "We could just plow through dumb old Adonis and his Water Warriors and get wherever we need to go."

"Not to drown your idea little dude, but I'm pretty sure a tank would not float," Pac said resting a hand on his friend's shoulder.

Sinking into a contemplative silence, the rest of the dinner finished without further discussions.

"I've been thinking about Noah's tank idea," Nina announced as Flynn made her way back to the breakfast table, bringing her back to the here and now.

"I was kind of kidding," Noah said sheepishly, not sure if he was embarrassed for himself or Nina.

"It doesn't matter if you were kidding or not," Professor Bebee said. "At this point, all ideas are welcome. What were you thinking Nina?"

"Well, it's kind of random, but I swear it connects, if you'll just hang with me until I finish."

"Go ahead dear," Professor Bebee said with a nod of her head in Nina's direction.

For the next few minutes Nina told a story about a

group of astronauts stranded in space and how a ground team of scientists helped to save their lives. The astronauts needed a filter to create breathable oxygen or they were going to die. To solve the problem the scientists on earth gathered a duplicate set of supplies to the ones on the spaceship, and used them to build a filter. Then, they told the astronauts what to do and how to do it. The astronauts built the filter, fixed their air supply problem and made it home safely.

"It was amazing! So I think we should do the same, with our junk, I mean stuff, here in the ARK. I think we should find everything we can, and build Noah's tank, or whatever will carry us to the Outlier Station," Nina finished, explaining breathlessly.

"It would be like the world's biggest science fair project ever," Flynn said.

"What's a science fair?" Noah asked.

"Never mind," Flynn said turning to look directly at Nina. The magic of a project was working its way into her veins. For a second, being with Nina was almost like being with Nora.

Nina smiled at Flynn and then broke their eye contact to look at Professor Bebee. "Can we do it?"

"We can, or we can die trying," Professor Bebee answered.

"I don't like your skepticism, but I'll take that as a yes," Flynn said determinedly.

"Don't be too stingy on those A's Professor B," Luke said from his position across the room. "If this is a school project, I want to pass."

"Getting to the Outlier Station will be your final test," Professor Bebee said, a smile hinting at the corners of her mouth.

"Does this mean we are building my tank?" Noah asked tentatively.

"Yes," Flynn said with a smile. "Yes, it most certainly

does. Now let's go find our junk to build it."

Chapter 7
Surface

"My heart is so tired." from: The Book Thief by Markus Zusak

    To enjoy the last of the holiday break before heading back to school, a majority of the Bay City High School population was mingling on the public beach. To an outsider, the scene wouldn't look much different than any other Saturday night in Bay City. Teenagers sat surrounding a bon fire, playing Frisbee in the waning sunlight, and talking over the Thanksgiving break.

    Tomorrow cliques would be reunited after a brief recess for obligatory family time. Classes would resume and plans for the new trimester would be made. Nora was still not sure if she was dreading it or craving it. Sitting next to her boyfriend Riley and Alex at the bon fire, she was spacing out, thinking about Flynn as usual. Talk of Savannah brought her out of her daze.

    "Do you remember the last time we were all together like this?" someone across the fire had said and an ominous silence fell upon the group. "And now that professor dude is missing too. Super weird."

    "Seriously," Nora muttered. "This is so not what I need." She got up and walked away from the fire. Alex followed her out to the shoreline. They stood at the edge of the beach, the tide inching up to their toes. "How could things get so messed up?" Nora asked, not really expecting an answer, although she wanted one badly.

    "I have no idea," Alex said not wanting the question to go unanswered either. After a minute he sighed and said,

    "Maybe we should just go to the surface scientists. Things have clearly gotten out of hand. Maybe we can't do it on our own."

"No," said Nora shaking her head, tears threatening to fall yet again. "They don't want us to. But I'm not sure how much longer they can be kept in the dark. I mean, don't you have to be smart to work there? How can they not tell that something is seriously wrong?"

"Well, we're doing a pretty good job of covering our trail. And when Simon comes back from break he'll be here to help. Have you talked to him lately?"

"He texted me earlier today. We are meeting at the Pit Stop during lunch on Monday. "

"Nora, are you even listening to yourself?" It was Riley. He had walked up behind them unnoticed. "Eating lunch at a gas station? Are you sure all of this is worth it? I mean you hardly do anything else anymore."

"Worth it? Riley! This is Flynn we are talking about!" Nora exclaimed.

"Yeah! And you're both sixteen!" Riley shot back. "I'm with Alex. I think it's time to turn it over to the professionals."

"Well thanks for your opinion, but I'm not taking it. I'm sticking to the plan."

"What plan?!" Riley burst out. "You don't even have a plan!"

"Right," Nora said locking tear stained eyes with him in the darkness. "Thanks for rubbing it in."

Nora turned away from the moonlit coast and marched toward the crowd around the fire. She didn't stop at the edge, but kept moving toward the street. Riley ran after her. Alex, sensing more drama than he cared to be a party to, walked back to the fire and sat down on the edge of a log. It wasn't long before Riley came huffing back to sit next to him.

"It's like I don't even know her anymore," Riley mumbled. "Dude, you gotta talk to her. You get this whole thing more than I do."

"Yeah, sure," Alex agreed. "No problem."

Or so he thought.

Chapter 8
Underwater Cave

"Fear is an acronym in the American Language for: False Evidence Appearing Real." – Neale David Walsch

"It is time to gather more warriors for our cause. We have work to do and need help to accomplish our goals." Adonis stopped talking and looked around the cave he now called home. He made a mental tally of the creatures present. *Mahi, Mackrels, Angelfish, Tuna, Threadfin… who is unaccounted for?* As if answering his question a silver swordfish swam to the entrance of the cave. Adonis gave a nod to the two sharks standing guard and the tardy commander was allowed to swim in. Adonis wasted no time seizing the opportunity in front of him and called the commander to come forward.

"As I look out across those that have gathered here, I can't help but notice, there are some not among us." Recognizing that the error in interrupting Adonis would only add to his tardy transgression Commander Dathan silently nodded. Adonis continued, "The jellyfish to name one. Their electrifying bodies would add the jolt our security system needs. Don't you agree commander?" Again the swordfish nodded. "Commander Dathan, I would like you to lead the search party. Talk with them, convince them to join us. Take a few of your pointy nosed friends along with you and see if you can't round up some new recruits."

"Yes Sir," Dathan finally spoke. Then he retreated back into the company of commanders.

Adonis searched the crowd again, contemplating his next selected "volunteer". A disturbance at the back of the cave distracted his decision making. A constant flow of dolphins were exiting the catacombs of the cave. Panicked chatter accompanied their presence into the chamber. An outburst of rage from Adonis silenced them immediately.

"What in Poseidon's blue ocean is happening?" he yelled. When no one responded he asked again, a forced calm in his voice. "What is going on here?"

"There has been a death," a brave soul spoke up.

"What do you mean?"

"In the labyrinth. In our caves. A fellow soldier didn't report for duty and when I went to check on him… he was gone."

"Not a death, a deserter! A traitor," Adonis accused.

"No, you don't understand."

"Well then explain it to me soldier before I entirely lose my patience because then there will be two dead soldiers to talk about."

"He… wasn't entirely gone. Pieces of him… remained. But… but he was… is no longer with us."

The gathered commanders turned to one another, discussing the situation. *Who could it have been? Is there a traitor among them? An assassin?* Their anxiety and conversation grated on Adonis' nerves, fraying them until he snapped.

"Silence!" The cave fell into an eerie hush. Adonis paced alone in front of the impromptu crowd. The militant creatures stood frozen, an underwater statue garden. "Double the guard. Everywhere. The traitor will not strike again. And Commander Dathan, security has now become an urgent matter. Don't delay or disappoint in your duty."

The scene of the murder was investigated and the remains were collected. For the first time Adonis' army understood the full effect of his fear inducing and action ceasing plan, because they now knew those feelings for themselves.

Chapter 9
ARK

"One man's trash is another man's treasure." – American Proverb

If they didn't think too hard about why they needed to search their deteriorating home for useful objects, it was almost fun. Almost. They could almost forget that building the tank was their only plan for success, almost deny that it was survival instincts that fueled their adrenaline rush instead of the game-like time requirement instilled before they departed to search. Almost.

They moved throughout the ARK in two's and three's and randomly grabbed items that might in some stretch of their imaginations become suddenly useful. They stuffed them into their collection bags or hauled them from room to room on their backs.

"This kind of reminds me of a scavenger hunt," Nina told Caspian and Noah as she flicked the switch of a desk lamp. Seeing it still worked, she coiled up the cord and tucked it in her bag. "Sometimes when we went to the beach my mom used to make up a list of all sorts of random things for us to find on the shore. Feathers, shells, seas glass, a pair of left behind sunglasses… and Nora and I would run up and down the beach searching for the items and putting them into our sand buckets. As I look back at it now, my mom probably just made up the lists so she could read her book on the beach in peace and quiet."

"Well I hypothesize it was a mutually beneficial event," Caspian commented.

"Yeah," Nina agreed smiling at the memory. "I guess it probably was."

Their search took them all over the ARK, visiting places

within their small world they hadn't laid eyes on in weeks: the labs, communication center, store rooms, closets and family pods. They visited them all and took from them what they could. Sooner than they felt fair, their two hour time allotment given by Professor Bebee expired. They all gathered again in the kitchen, dragging their treasures in behind them. Piles of objects lay on every available surface. Air filters, empty oxygen tanks, rope, nets, fish collection baskets and an assortment of other objects littered the tables. As they entered the kitchen Professor Sorenson was directing them to sort their items into three different piles: Things that float, things that could be manipulated to create movement and things for creating an outer shell of a vehicle.

Once all of the items had been divided according to their chief purpose, the crew members were divided as well. Flynn, Professor Sorenson and Anton, who refused to be in a group with Caspian were to work with the creating movement objects, attempting to create some sort of propulsion system. Sonora, Stillman, Professor Bebee and Caspian looked at the objects able to float and were calculating how much weight they could safely support. That left Noah, Luke, Pac and Nina to create the cavity of the tank.

"If we can create the world's best underwater sport, we can definitely build a tank," Luke encouraged.

"Totally," Pac agreed. "Plus, it's obvious they gave us the job with all the heavy lifting because we are so buff," he added flexing.

"I'm sure that's what they were thinking," Nina teased with a laugh.

"Come on! Let's get to work!" Noah piped in excitedly.

A few hours later they sat surrounded by pieces of random objects, no closer to creating a tank than Adonis was to inviting the crew to a pleasant picnic in the park. The thrill and excitement of the project was starting to wear off.

"I don't know why we thought we could do this," Nina

said. "I'm sorry I even suggested it."

"Don't beat yourself up," Pac said. "It was a good idea. We just couldn't pull it off."

"If only we had, like a... pre-made box... that we could just add on to," Noah whined.

"Wait! What did you just say?" Luke asked.

"A box, like, already made. Something to just build off of, instead of starting from scratch," Noah further explained.

"Huh. Interesting."

"Interesting how bro?" Pac asked sensing there was more to his buddy's vocalized musing.

"I might have an idea," Luke continued.

"Well don't keep us in suspense!" Nina said, her annoyance masked by a nervous laugh.

"Follow me." Luke stood and walked out of the kitchen. The rest of his cavity crew followed him out of the door, down the hall and into the loading dock. Pac marched over to the TUBE and pressed the UP button. When the doors opened he dramatically swept his arms, gesturing to the passenger compartment of the TUBE.

"Ta-da!" Luke said, a wide signature grin on his face. "Now, all we have to do is get it out of there, make it move inconspicuously through the water and we'll all get A's for sure."

* * * * * *

They wasted no time. Removing the passenger chamber from the TUBE was a difficult and multi-stepped project. First, to avoid flooding the ARK, the TUBE needed to be completely drained of water. It was decided that this would happen at night to elude the attention of the Surface Station staff. Plus, Simon wasn't getting back into town until after dinner and they couldn't accomplish this task without him.

Simon had briefly entertained the idea of inviting Nora along on the nocturnal foray, but then remembered it was a school night, so abandoned the idea. Instead he had forwarded her the email he'd received from Professor Sorenson and told her he'd fill her in on all she missed tomorrow at lunch. She didn't argue.

Using his key card, Simon swiped himself into the station praying no one would check the door log to notice his unauthorized presence late at night. He fumbled through the dark building to his "office". At once the familiar space set him at ease and he began meticulously following the instructions sent to him.

The water slowly gurgled and bubbled its way out of the TUBE in a controlled and pressurized stream. It flowed out of the TUBE, over the metal grated floor of the loading dock into the water collection tank and was then deposited into the ocean. Simon oversaw the operation from above, while Flynn and Professor Sorenson supervised below. A yellow light alerted Simon when the drainage was complete. He flicked the hibernation switch that activated the air filter system to rid the TUBE of any residual moisture, avoiding potential mold growth. Once his part in the clandestine activity was complete, he silently slipped out of the station. On his walk home he texted Nora. *Another job for the good guys done. TUBE empty and dry. Gnight. See u 2morrow.*

When the message buzzed her phone, Nora groggily leaned out of bed to check it, smiled and fell back to sleep.

Chapter 10
Surface

"Don't let what you can't do interfere with what you can do."
– John Wooden

Nora sat in a booth of the diner attached to the gas station. She absent-mindedly fed French fry after French fry into her mouth, only pausing to dip each one into ketchup. Through the window she saw Simon ride up on his bike, wearing a Bay City University sweatshirt and matching stocking cap. She distractedly wondered if the waitress would think they were on a lunch date, before she quickly dismissed the idea because Simon was far too dorky to even be considered boyfriend material. Simon locked up his bike and came into the diner. Eyeing Nora, he walked over and took a seat opposite her in the booth.

"Take off that hat," Nora said brusquely.

"It' cold." Simon's voice came out in an almost whine.

"It's obvious. It's memorable. Take it off."

Simon's hand crept up to his crown and sheepishly removed the hat, revealing an untamed mane of reddish hair.

"So what's the status update at the Surface Station? I mean other than the dry, empty TUBE. Do they like, have a clue what is going on?" Nora asked, pushing her empty plastic fry basket away.

"I stopped by there on my way here. They told me to go to my work station right away because there would probably be a lot of requests piling up since I had been on break for the past week. Clearly they hadn't noticed anything out of the ordinary, while I was gone. But when I got to my desk, it was just how I left it. So I quickly filled out a bunch of fake request slips and spread them out. I added a few coupons for some typically requested items and a couple of post it notes for good measure. They only way someone will know they are fake is if they stop to look at the handwriting."

"Good. Good thinking," Nora said and Simon beamed in her meager praise. "How long until you think they'll figure out the TUBE is broken?"

"Well, right before all this craziness started one of the surface scientists taught me how to retrieve the requests and send back the cargo. So unless actual people are going down to the ARK, I should be the only one who needs to check it."

"Is there a calendar posted somewhere, so we can figure out when someone might be planning on going down?" Nora asked.

Reaching into the front pocket of his hooded BCU sweatshirt Simon produced the very item Nora requested. He had gotten good at delivering what people needed. Nora looked at him from across the table, genuinely impressed. This time she silently applauded his efforts with a smile and Simon blushed. Nora paged through the calendar and her polished finger landed on December 31.

"There is supposed to be this elegant New Year's Gala. Big time donors, University big wigs – all heading down to ring in a new year of scientific progress," Simon explained. "I was already given a list by Mrs. Worthington of items to start stock piling for the party."

While Nora sat in silent contemplation Simon said (mostly to himself), "I… was hoping I could go." Nora looked up at him and he continued, "Not as a guest or anything. A butler maybe? I just… I really wanted to see it, the ARK."

"I have never once wished to go down there," Nora said coldly. "But I do love a good party. And a chandelier lit gala under the sea does sound pretty amazing."

"Yeah, well, not like it's going to happen anymore now huh?" Simon asked.

"No, probably not. But we can't let anyone else know

that," Nora said, all business again.

"Right," Simon agreed, shaking off his daydream. "But how?"

"For starters, hang the calendar back up before someone notices it missing and starts asking questions. Keep buying the items Mrs. What's-her-name tells you to, along with any other party planning task she tells you to do." Simon nodded with each instruction Nora gave. "Keep submitting requests for the daily items, but hold off really buying the items. Just hang on to that money. I don't know what we'll need it for yet. But it's always good to have a stash of cash for emergencies."

"Okay," Simon said. "That sounds good. Really, I don't think it will be that hard to fool them. Everyone is all freaked out about Professor Sorenson going missing. It seems like all projects got put on hold once he disappeared. Like they can't more forward without his permission, so they just aren't doing anything. Some of the staff aren't even coming into the station anymore."

"That's good news for us," Nora said before taking a final slurp of her water. "Flynn left her converter-thingy here so we could communicate. She is supposed to be calling me tonight. I'll email you afterward if there is any new info."

"What'll it be loves?" a gum snapping waitress asked.

"Actually, I'm out. Sixth period starts in like eight minutes." Nora stood. "This should cover mine," she said laying a few bills on the table.

"Okay. Um, bye," Simon said.

"See ya," Nora said, already half way across the diner.

Simon watched her run-walk across the parking lot and through the crosswalk onto the Bay City High School Campus before turning back to the still gum chomping waitress to order his lunch. Undercover work was strenuous and he had worked up an appetite.

Twenty five minutes and two double cheeseburger

baskets later he sighed with satisfaction. He also needed to get back to class. If he could bike his bloated belly at a decent speed, he had just enough time to return the calendar to the Surface Station before Marine Bio 101.

Chapter 11
ARK

"Girls we love for what they are; young men for what they promise to be." – Johann Wolfgang von Goethe

It was nearly impossible for Nina and Caspian to keep up their nightly post-dinner ritual, but they tried their best. Every evening they would discretely retreat to the edge of the kitchen, now common room, and look out the door toward the observation deck. The view wasn't as good as they were used to, but the company more than made up for it.

Their days were thick with the present. These nightly discussions belonged to the past and future: memories and dreams, traditions and plans. Without even trying, their futures entwined until one was inseparable from the other.

A four year university, post graduate humanitarian travels and volunteering, Thanksgiving at the Nelson's and Christmas in the ARK. It was a nice little life they had planned for themselves, and they wallowed in their dream world future – refusing to let current circumstances dissuade them of its possibility.

For everyone else, the scene was nothing new, but Flynn marveled at the creature who used to be her familiar brother. She was happy for him, but she couldn't stomach watching him tuck Nina's brown hair behind her ear even one more time. She moved from her place at the dinner table to a spot completely across the room.

Noah and Pac were playing a newly invented card game that resembled "go fish", but was somehow transformed into a much livelier rendition. Luke watched from the sidelines both attempting to learn the made up rules and suggest new ones. The professors sat talking quietly while

Sonora and Stillman could be seen down at the obscoral tank chatting with Jett. As usual, Anton sat alone, the absence of Carl never more visible than it was in the crew's rare free time.

    A shiver raced across Flynn's skin as she sat down on a cool metal chair. A mountain range of goose bumps rose on her arms and legs, a northern and southern ridge. A memory unbidden flashed across her mind. She was sitting on the Florida sun-soaked curb – chipped yellow paint and all – waiting for Mr. Nelson to pick her and Nora up. The pavement, sometimes hot to the touch, was warming her from the outside-in as she and Nora discussed the day's events, squinting against the setting sun as they looked for their minivan chariot. Unconsciously a smile found its way to her face and Luke said,

    "Penny for your thoughts." As he wandered over to her away from the game, she had to physically shake the memory from her head.

    "It was nothing," she responded.

    "What do you miss the most?" Luke asked taking up a spot on the floor next to her chair.

    "A thousand little things," she answered without hesitation. "A full moon reflecting off the surface of the ocean, the chirp of cicadas, the smell of anything not manmade, but especially the smell of a bonfire."

    "I've never told anyone this, but sometimes, I dream about the surface. It's always the same, one night, camping. Singing around a bonfire, marshmallows. I think that's why I love to play guitar. Because it reminds of those happy summer nights."

    "I forgot you played," Flynn said, looking down at him.

    "It's been so long since I have, I almost forgot too."

    "You would have liked the surface. Especially the parties. I swear every single one was outside. Underneath the night sky with a thousand stars shinning down on you. It felt like anything could happen."

"After this month, I'm not so sure that sounds like a good thing."

"I know, but before all of this mess, it was the best feeling in the world. And Nora. You would have LOVED Nora."

"Was she like you?"

"We are like twins separated at birth."

"Then I'm sure you're right." He looked up at her with his crystal clear blue eyes and for a second she could think of nothing else.

"Well," she stammered, breaking the silence, "we'll go back and you can meet her then. Promise me we'll go back," Flynn demanded fiercely.

"I promise," Luke whispered. And she believed him.

Chapter 12
Surface

"Walking with a friend in the dark is better than walking alone in the light." – Hellen Keller

Nora sat propped up in bed, her computer's glowing screen coming to life on her lap. Despite the dire situation, she was calmer and happier than she had been in weeks. Talking to a best friend can definitely have that effect on a girl. Now, all she had to do was boil a giddy and frantic half-hour conversation down into a useful and informative email.

She stared at the blinking cursor for a minute, then took a deep breath and began typing.

Simon,

I talked to Flynn tonight. Here is their plan and what they need us to do.

1. They are in the process of building a submarine-like vehicle from scratch so they can travel to some place called the Outlier Station. Apparently they think it is in better condition and stocked with more supplies. Flynn also said they are hoping that the missing adults are there as well. (Cross your fingers!) The submarine isn't done yet, but they are hoping within a few days, it will be.
2. They haven't totally decided their next plan of action yet. (Flynn said trying to get scientists to commit to a project is worse that forcing me to select a single pair of shoes to take on vacation – which would never happen, so I totally understand her frustration at having to wait) ANYWAY, they are "strongly thinking" about "starting to work" on an antidote to the whole fish talking problem. They might need us to hook them up with some supplies stashed at the Surface

> Station for this part. I told Flynn you were a master delivery man, so it shouldn't be a problem.

And that's pretty much it. I told her about the New Year's Gala and how we are doing our best to make sure things look normal. And I was right. I would have totally loved that party. Flynn said its easily in the top 3 best parts about living in the ARK. Eventually the idiots at the Surface Station will see what has been in front of their noses for weeks, but let's prolong that blessed little discovery as long as we possibly can.

Meet me at the PitStop on Friday at 11:30 and we can check in with any new info we have. If you need me before then, just email.

Later,
Nora

    She read the email through twice and then clicked send. As she slid her laptop under her bed and snuggled into her covers she thought about what she hadn't said in the email. She hadn't told Simon that for the first five minutes of the call Nora and Flynn had squealed and giggled and shrieked at decibels of happiness only teenage girls can understand. She didn't tell him that it had taken Caspian a solid two minutes of trying to interrupt them to get the conversation on track. She didn't tell him that after all the business was discussed Flynn had snuck away and hid in the kitchen pantry while they talked about Nora's first day at school without her. They talked about Alex and Riley and Savannah and the ruinous relationships of all three. She didn't tell him that when it was time to end the call they both cried.
    Neither girl would admit it out loud to the scientific brains that surrounded them, but those last moments of secret, scandalously unproductive time spent socializing had been more beneficial to their sanity than anything else that had been discussed that night.

* * * * * *

Across town at a lamp lit desk Simon heard the chime of his email inbox and minimized an internet search window. He had been doing some research on the Pollution Eating Solution that had turned his life upside down – in a good way. All his life he had been distracted, a jumbled mess. Now he had a cause on which to focus all that restless and wasted energy. Sure he was still occasionally clumsy, and his ear buds still had a permanent place dangling around his neck, but he was different. He was on time and organized and prepared. And because of those things he was gaining confidence and finally excelling at his four year university of choice.

He clicked on the email from Nora and read it in the silence of his empty dorm room. As soon as he was finished he added Nora's meeting at the PitStop to the calendar app on his phone and then went back to the research article. He thought he might try to identify the supplies Nora hinted at, not wanting to depreciate his ability to deliver. He thought there was a good chance they could be found at the Surface Station, but if not there, maybe in a bio lab supply closet at school. He decided it wouldn't hurt to get a head start and be ready when the time came.

His eyes scanned page after page of articles and reports written by Professor Sorenson and Dr. Brinestone. His hand flew across his notebook page, listing what he deemed important. *Just one more article, one more lab report, one more press release* he told himself. One turned into three, turned into ten, turned into… he lost count. But he did know that his roommate had long ago stumbled into the room and had been snoring for quite some time. He took that as a cue to call it a night. As his computer shutdown he rubbed his tired eyes with his knuckles and debated falling asleep right there in his chair. In the end he flopped on to the futon not two feet away and fell asleep instantly.

Chapter 13
ARK

Now I'll be bold
As well as strong
And use my head alongside my heart.
So take my flesh
And fix my eyes
A tethered mind freed from the lies.
- *I Will Wait, Mumford and Sons*

    Caspian and 'Cuda continued to meet twice daily, at first and last light. Speaking in soft voices they shared information in the safe sheltered space beneath the loading dock. 'Cuda floated just outside the window where Caspian pressed as close as possible to hear the words from his fishy friend.

    This morning 'Cuda was accompanied by a large sea turtle. The male turtle loomed just beyond 'Cuda, his brown and white mosaicked flippers moving slightly as he treaded water in place. His almond shaped dark eyes darted between their meeting place and the wide expanse of open-ocean behind him. Despite his anxiety, he floated patiently while Caspian gave a quick brief on yesterday's progress on the submarine and 'Cuda gave the daily scouting report. Then conversation steered toward the newcomer.

    "Caspian, this is Kurma. He has come with a proposition for you. I believe he can be trusted," 'Cuda said by way of introduction.

    "'Cuda has told me about your vehicle and your plan to leave this place to survey another building about a mile from here." Caspian nodded while the turtle talked wondering where the conversation was headed. "We would like to offer our services. We would be willing to tow your vehicle to the Outlier Station."

"Not that I am ungrateful, but why do you want to help us?" Caspian asked.

"Adonis' brutality continues to grow. Anyone who refuses to join him is a target for violence. We have not been approached yet, but it is only a matter of time. My herd and I, would like to avoid both joining him and his bullying." Caspian appeared deep in thought. Kurma continued. "Hopefully by helping you achieve this intermediary goal, it will increase your chances of overall success, therefore returning us all to our natural state. We are also hoping that in helping you, you will agree to protect us in any way you can. As I'm sure you know, we need to return to the surface often to breathe. At first we passed through the sunlight zone unharmed, but yesterday and again this morning, some of our group was attacked. We need a source of fresh air we can turn to when the attacks increase and traveling to the surface becomes too dangerous."

Caspian sat, seriously thinking through the offer presented. "You are very wise, Kurma. How old are you?"

"I've had many years to gather this wisdom, although only a few weeks to share this wisdom, as you call it, aloud with human speech."

"I will consider your offer and also take it back to the crew for discussion. I cannot commit without speaking to them first. I will also try to think of a solution to your oxygen problem."

"Now you, Captain Caspian, are showing your own wisdom," complimented Kurma.

"Thank you," Caspian said, ducking his head in acknowledgment of the praise.

"To show our loyalty in this matter I have already sent two spies to your Outlier Station. They will report back to me by last light the condition of the building and if any humans reside inside."

At this last bit of news Caspian's heart raced. He almost wanted to seal the deal right here and now, but he remembered Kurma's praise and his decision to discuss the proposal with the rest of the crew. With effort he restrained himself from diving into the alliance without consent. For some reason unknown to him, Caspian sought the approval of this old wise soul. He hypothesized this was what having a grandfather might feel like.

"Thank you," Caspian finally responded. "for coming to us and for your offer. I hope we can work together. We will meet back here again at last light for progress and status reports. Until then, swim safe, swim strong."

'Cuda and Kurma nodded and then silently swam away, leaving Caspian to sit alone in the sterile loading dock, long ago empty of supplies and cargo. He thought, not for the first time since this ordeal began, what his father would do if he were in this situation. He reasoned that his father would calmly present the offer and any known facts to the crew and then allow for ample discussion. Caspian decided he would like to do the same, but with a submarine to build, an antidote to create and general survival on the daily agenda he wasn't confident in his ability to provide the abundant discussion and think time that the situation warranted.

"Well, sitting here wasting time thinking about it isn't going to put more time on the clock," Caspian told himself. He heaved himself off the floor with a big sigh only to instantly sink back down to his spot of safety, arms thrown over his head.

"Holy sea silt Anton! You scared the kelp out of me," Caspian uncharacteristically swore.

"Sorry. I didn't mean to," Anton said, though neither his tone nor his face showed any sign of remorse. "Look, I'm not gonna lie to you. I was purposely eavesdropping."

"Why?" Caspian asked, voice thick with confusion.

"Your last plan most likely got my best friend killed. So

forgive me for not jumping on board wit every plan to make!"

"I'm sorry, I-"

"This place feels like a monarchy. Ruled by the professors and you. For the rest of us – it's like our opinions don't count, or worse, aren't even consulted. I get it, you're the oldest, the next Brinestone prodigy. But it's our lives too man." A vein on Anton's forehead throbbed, peeking out from under his curly black hair.

"Anton, I know, I-"

"Yeah," Anton interrupted. "You do know. And now I know you know. But I needed proof. I had to be sure."

"Well, okay." Caspian said, his breathing finally returning to normal. "So now what?"

"We go tell the rest of the crew what Mr. Loggerhead said and see what they have to say."

"Your vote?" Caspian asked tentatively.

"I'm all in on this one." Anton reached out a hand and pulled Caspian up from the floor. Together they walked toward the kitchen, for once, a front united.

Chapter 14
Surface

"The ache for home lives in all of us, the safe place we can go as we are and not be questioned." – Maya Angelou

Everyone noticed Flynn's absence from school on Monday. Some assumed she was just home sick. Nora had briefly overheard a rumor in the girl's bathroom that Flynn had eaten some bad turkey and was now home puking her guts out. Nora didn't bother to set them straight. She almost wished it were true.

A few asked Nora directly as to Flynn's whereabouts and when she told them she had been called back home to help with a family crisis, they all expressed their overwhelming teenage sadness. In a way, Nora thought it was nice to be able to commiserate with people who felt the trauma at the same level she did. On the other hand, her plan for escaping the doom and gloom of Flynn's exit from her life, completely bit the dust.

It wasn't until Tuesday, a full day after the news had broken that Kelsey wielded the situation and her new #1 mean girl status for an attack. It happened, as all school drama does, in one of those unstructured moments of the school day. As Nora stood in the ala carte food line (alone ☹) Kelsey launched her assault.

"Where's your sidekick soccer girl? Still enjoying the benefits of being food poisoned by your mom's Thanksgiving cooking?"

Nora turned to look at her, venom in her eyes, but not a hint of emotion in her voice.

"There are so many things wrong with that statement, I'm not even going to reply. You might want to tell your little minions to work on their fact checking skills."

"Clearly you are the one who's got something wrong. You look like crap."

"Why thank you for noticing. You on the other hand look positively amazing. Isn't that Savannah's skirt? Really Kelsey, stealing from your best friend, who's currently considered a missing person by the Bay City Police Department? Talk about a fashion crime."

Nora set down her ala carte items and left the speechless girl behind her, left the cafeteria lines behind her, left the BCHS campus entirely behind her. She didn't stop walking until she sat down across from Simon in a vinyl covered booth at the PitStop.

"We didn't plan to –"

"Rough day. Had to get outta there."

"Oh."

"Do you eat here every day?" Nora asked him not sure whether she was judging him or if she had misjudged the PitStop.

"Creature of habit," he said with a shrug. "Plus, the double cheeseburgers are to die for."

Chapter 15
ARK

"A person wants to believe in folks and trust in things, and when you can't – life doesn't seem worth living anymore." – Piper McCloud from: <u>The Girl Who Could Fly</u> by Victoria Forester

The last rays of light were rapidly retreating, leaving the ARK in darkening shadows. Caspian sat watching the light race toward the surface as he waited for the return of 'Cuda and Kurma. He knew he was early and he knew why. He was anxious to hear the old turtle's report about the Outlier Station. If there was a chance he could get the information even a minute sooner, he wanted to take advantage of the opportunity.

He was also anxious to report his own news. The crew had unanimously decided to accept the sea turtles' offer. In the first place, ARK allies had been few and far between, not to mention hard to come by. Turning down an olive branch from even one species seemed foolish. Secondly, work on the submarine's structure was soaring ahead, but without Carl, the mechanical engineering was leaving lots to be desired. If they could count on the towing service of the turtles, their vehicle must only need to hold humans and float above the sea floor, which seemed a much more manageable task. All of these factors overwhelmingly pointed in favor of accepting the turtles' proposal, and so they did.

But all of those thoughts fled Caspian's mind as 'Cuda and Kurma swam up to the portal window. Caspian's heart was in his throat and he was afraid if he spoke, more than words would come out. Instead he stared at the two creatures waiting for them to speak first.

"We bring good news," 'Cuda said, wanting to erase

the helpless look on his friend's face.

"My scouts have reported human activity at the Outlier Station," Kurma reported and Caspian released a breath he hadn't known he was holding. "It appears they are maintaining survival, but are being daily harassed by Adonis and his followers."

"We call them the Water Warriors," Caspian interjected.

"A good name. They are fierce and bold. We think they come to the building at scheduled times, so with a little more surveillance we can use that information to help us when selecting the time we approach."

"Excellent," Caspian replied, the relief apparent on his face. "Thank you."

"We have fulfilled our promise to you and shown the depth of our loyalty," Kurma said. "What have you decided about our offer of alliance?"

"I have already spoken in favor of you joining our cause and council," 'Cuda said surveying both parties. "Caspian, what do you and the crew have to say?"

"We say yes. Absolutely yes."

"Wonderful. Thank you."

"I wish I had more than words to give you. You have already given us so much." Caspian continued, "All I can say, is I promise to devote time to finding you a safe breathing space. We could entertain the idea of bringing you inside. We have the space... and tanks. 'Cuda I've actually been wanting to discuss this with you too. I don't feel right about sitting in here safe and sound while you are out there exposed."

"I don't mean to speak for the barracuda," Kurma began. "but we don't want to be your pets."

"I didn't mean to offend you, I was only trying to –"

"We know," said the turtle, dipping his pointed nose in honor. "But all the same. We wish to remain outside, free from constraints."

"Even if that means being in danger? Possibly dying?" Caspian asked.

"It is our choice," Kurma insisted.

'Cuda nodded toward Caspian. "I feel the same, but thank you. Really, don't worry, I have a safe place to stay."

Caspian nodded. "Alright. But if you change your mind, please know, you are welcome. Always welcome."

The three said their good nights and departed their separate ways, hearts heavy, but minds clinging to their new found shred of hope.

Chapter 16
Underwater Cave

*"I'm trapped in a nightmare where nothing makes sense." – from:
<u>The Neptune Project</u> by Polly Holyoke*

"Why me? Why listen to one dolphin in all of the ocean?" Adonis questioned.

"Because you are the one who stood up and spoke when the time was right," a voice rose up from the depths. Adonis had so little sleep he was unsure if he was answering his own question or if a god of the sea was guiding his thoughts and actions. Neither was true.

"I will rest," he told himself.

"There is no time for rest," the voice urged. "Press on to victory. Tomorrow enjoy the peace that comes with success."

"Yes. Yes, tomorrow," Adonis repeated numbly.

"What did you say Sir?" Marianus asked, swimming into the cavern.

"Nothing. Just talking to myself. What news do you bring?"

"There have been two more deaths in the labyrinth. The soldiers are ready to riot. Something needs to be done or you will have a mutiny on your fins." Adonis sighed, weary of the troubles on his list as a leader.

"I will take care of it," Adonis promised.

"By yourself? But how?" Marianus questioned.

"Do not doubt me. I said I will take care of it and I will."

"Yes Sir. It's only that you look so tired."

"Rest is for the weak!" Adonis snapped. "Leave me before I delegate you to deal with the duty of exposing this traitorous murderer."

"Yes sir." Marianus swam out of the cavern leaving his leader physically, but his mind remained in the cave, pondering the many questions that swam in his brain.

Chapter 17
ARK

"Do not mess with someone else's feeling just because you are unsure of yours." – from: The #44 Rule of a Lady by muppetandco.blogspot.nl

Once the TUBE passenger compartment had been extracted, the submarine project came together at a remarkable speed. Beads of melted metal were welded to every corner, crevice and adjoining edge and then the entire encasement was painted with a waterproof sealer. Empty aluminum oxygen tanks were affixed to the bottom, a silver row of flotation units. Together Flynn and Professor Sorenson had rigged up a filter to use its water flow to help the submarine hover ever so slightly off the sea floor.

When the initial construction was completed, Flynn noted that while it would do its job, the submarine wasn't the prettiest fish in the pond. It was Stillman who then recommended they cover the vehicle with seaweed to act as camouflage.

Pac and Luke volunteered to retrieve the green foliage from the ARK farm, but when one of them was needed to operate the lift gate to submerge their submarine in the obscoral tank for a trial run, Flynn offered to go in Pac's place. No one had been to the aqua farm in a long time. Once the crew had gathered all that had been currently edible they left it to manage itself. After the whirlpool had devastatingly damaged it, they didn't even know if it was safe to enter. But given the alternative – a potentially dangerous and leaking room inside the ARK was considerably safer than the enemy infested waters outside it.

The pair double checked the oxygen levels and extent

of any flooding before deeming the farm section safe to enter. They sloshed through rows and rows of water logged crops, rotting past the point of practical use. In the center of the farm lay a salt water aquifer filled with an abundance of still fresh seaweed. Wasting no time, they got to work.

    Luke would hoist the crop out from the water and Flynn would cut it off at the roots. They then placed it in a pile on an outstretched cargo net they brought to carry their load. Hoist, cut, pile. Hoist, cut, pile. Flynn got a little carried away with a load while hefting it into the pile and seaweed slapped Luke clean across the face. He lost his balance and fell flat on his butt, in the pooling water. Flynn reached out an arm and helped him up, the two of them suddenly laughing uncontrollably. They sat down on the edge of the aquifer tank to rest.

    "Sorry about that," Flynn giggled, and picked a piece of seaweed out of Luke's shaggy hair.

    "No worries," Luke said. Once he stopped laughing and his breathing returned to normal he added, "It wasn't the same without you."

    "Yeah, Noah told me a serious amount of morning bathroom time opened up in our family pod," Flynn responded nonchalantly, staring past the rows of the farm, through the glass walls, as if trying to see all the way back up to the surface.

    "That wasn't what I meant. I," Luke paused. "I missed you. I'm glad you're back."

    Flynn didn't know what to say. *I'm not. I thought of you only when running with the dog, who happened to have the same name. What did you just say?* Instead she said, "I think we can fit about four more arm loads of seaweed in that net and then we should get back."

    "You're right," Luke said standing up. "They'll be waiting for us."

    They harvested the rest of the needed seaweed,

working in an efficient tandem silence. When the cargo net was filled to the bursting they pushed and pulled it back through the rows of crops, out of the farm and down the halls. They left a slick wet trail, as well as their awkward moment behind them.

Chapter 18
Surface

"When we talk about settling the world's problems, we're barking up the wrong tree. The world is perfect. It's a mess. It has always been a mess. We are not going to change it. Our job is to straighten out our own lives." – Joseph Campbell

"Alex will you do me a favor?" Nora asked.

They were sitting on the pier, waiting for Riley to be done mastering level 47 on his favorite video game at the arcade.

"That's a loaded question these days."

"No, no. Nothing like that. Nothing top secret, I promise. It's just, I've been eating lunch with Simon. Every day."

"Everyday?" Alex almost choked on his smoothie they had ordered from the Smoothie Shak on their way.

"At the PitStop. And – I don't want him to think we are… that it's like dating. Or like, think I like, like him."

"Ahhh, that kind of a favor. Why don't you ask Riley?" As soon as he'd asked the question Riley whooped in glee at successfully completing the level. He pantomimed begging for five more minutes and Nora smiled, nodded and then rolled her eyes at Alex.

"He doesn't have the same lunch period as me. I don't want to hurt Simon's feelings. So, could you please just come along? Tomorrow? A couple times a week?"

"Sure. But why don't you just eat in the cafeteria?"

"Ugh. I can't handle it there. Kelsey and her mean girl minions, memories of Flynn. Please? Please say you'll come?" Nora begged.

"Well…" Alex playfully stalled.

"11:30. Promise me."

"Okay. You know I can't say no to you."

"Oh Alex! You're the best!" Nora threw her arms around her him, smothering him in a big hug. "Now, let's go get Riley and drag his butt home for dinner."

* * * * * * *

Nora walked into her house just as the evening news was coming on. She took a seat at the kitchen island and listened while her mother silently continued to prepare dinner.

"Lots of sad stories filling the news today," crooned a middle aged woman.

"Yes, Darla, you're right about that," said her co-anchor, Dallas sympathetically.

"We'll start with the discovery of a body on the beach. The body of a male teenager was found on a stretch of beach near the University's Surface Station. The boy carried no identification and his description matches no missing person's reports. What is even stranger is that no one has even come to look at the body to try and claim it," Darla reported.

"A mystery waiting to be solved," added Dallas.

"Indeed. Now, we are hoping this image is not too graphic for our home audience, but here is a picture of the boy. If you know him, or have any information on who he might be, please contact the station or the police immediately."

"Join us, Dallas and Darla, News 7 Evening Crew, after this short commercial break for news on the continued hunt for two missing persons, a teenager and a local university professor."

Click.

Nora turned off the TV and walked out of the kitchen wishing she could leave her own problems behind as easily.

Chapter 19
Underwater Cave

"It is better to be hated for what you are, than loved for what you are not." – from: The Autumn Leaves by Andre Gide

"Commander Dathan! Report forward to debrief." The swordfish swam slowly forward. He turned his back to his peers and faced Adonis. "Have you succeeded in your task?"

"I'm afraid I have bad news to report," Commander Dathan began. "We were unable to convince the jellyfish to join our side. It was a fool's errand in the first place. The humans have a jellyfish within their bubble whom they've already befriended. I'm sorry to say the jellyfish have decided to side against us."

"Well you are right about one thing. You are a fool. A fool to believe that I would buy that ridiculous story."

"Sir, I-"

"Enough! Tell me no more lies," Adonis' voice reverberated off the cave walls. He began to circle Commander Dathan, berating him at every turn. "You, with your built-in pointy weaponry couldn't convince, recruit, bully those spineless water windsocks to join us? You were right about another thing as well. You should be afraid. Very afraid." Adonis ceased his circling and fell back a few paces. "Guards? Kill him." The sharks descended on the unsuspecting fish with incredible speed, catching him completely unaware and defenseless.

When the deed was done, Dathan's scales and point were stripped and fashioned into a sword and armor. Then Adonis stood in front of them, clad in his new panoply. Silence permeated the cave. Terrified at the sight, but afraid to look away, the commanders watched and waited for their leader's next move.

"My new suit of armor. Do you like it? Would you like some?" When no one answered he supplied one for them, "I think we should all have some."

"Admiral Marianus!"

"Admiral Sir?" A Mahi separated himself from the crowd and swam forward.

"You've just been promoted."

"Thank you, Sir."

"And with your new rank comes new responsibility."

"What would you have me do, Sir?"

"Our warriors need to be ready for battle. This includes being fitted properly. Take care of it."

"I'm not sure I understand," Marianus said.

Adonis flicked his shiny new sword through the water so that its tip landed under the Mahi's blue green chin. "The Water Warriors must be suited for battle. Take care of it Admiral."

"Yes sir."

"Oh and Admiral, take the sharks. As you've just seen, their sharp teeth will prove helpful."

*   *   *   *

A black and yellow angelfish sliced through the night black water. His tiny heart pumped hard from the exertion of speed and fear. His nose pushed through the vines and once he swam a few feet forward he could feel their presence on all sides of him. His eyes darted back and forth hoping to land on the form of a silver fish instead of one of the poisonous snakes he knew to live there. Surprisingly the vines did feel like they offered a small amount of protection. His heart began to slow along with his pace as he inched further and further into the League of the Dark Vines. Without warning the vines cleared and as if by magic or miracle, 'Cuda floated, waiting in its center.

"Trouble," Hale spat out.

"I suspected," 'Cuda replied.

"Adonis has sent a unit to ambush the swordfish. He wants them dead."

"Why?" Shock and horror evident in the barracuda's voice.

"Betrayal and armor," Hale dutifully answered.

"I don't understand."

"Dathan reported he was unable to sway the jellyfish to join Adonis. But really, he never tried. He had decided to trade teams. We talked about it a few days ago. Double crossing Adonis and securing the jellyfish as ARK allies were his first acts of deception. He paid for it dearly." Hale's eyes communicated the words he didn't say aloud.

"Not the first. Not the last. Not in vain," 'Cuda assured the small fish.

"They will never see it coming. Most of the swordfish think Adonis their friend. They don't know Dathan was turning sides. He was trying to protect them… keeping them in the dark," Hale reported to 'Cuda.

"In the end, it was his secrets that will hurt them most," 'Cuda commented.

"Sadly, you're right. Maybe it is better that Dathan isn't around to see how this all turns out."

"He was a good fish, caught in a bad current. I will report all of this to Caspian. I'm not sure what he'll be able to do, but I know he will want to help. What else can you tell me?" 'Cuda asked.

"Not much. Adonis only tells us information at the very last minute."

"Is he trying to decide what to do? Having trouble making up his mind?"

"It could be, but I don't think so. I think he is afraid of spies and deserters. By keeping us in the dark, he is able to limit those traitorous actions."

"Good thing there are none of those," 'Cuda said smiling and winking in an attempt to make light of the heavy situation.

"Good thing," Hale said, his smile more forced. "I should get going, but I'll report back when I can."

"Swim safe. Swim strong."

Hale repeated the motto and then left the League of the Dark Vines, swimming back to duty and danger.

Chapter 20
Surface

"She was saying goodbye and she didn't even know it." – from: <u>The Book Thief</u> by Markus Zusak

    Nora had never been much of a reader. She usually left that to Nina, but now the far away worlds pressed between the paperback covers of her sister's books held a new appeal. In fact, she almost preferred to live through the characters' drama than her own. Instead of venturing out after her homework was done as she used to do, Mr. and Mrs. Nelson often found her curled up on the couch reading. Silently they'd nod at each other and congratulate themselves on reigning in their dramatic daughter and turning her into a well-rounded child.

    But tonight her novel in progress lay lonely on the coffee table and Nora stood in line next to Riley waiting to buy their tickets for the game. It was the home opener for the boys' basketball team and half the town had shown up to see the Bay City Barracudas take on their cross team rivals. Pockets of maroon and gold could be seen amidst the sea of blue and silver, and Nora and Riley stood in the center of it all – not talking. Shuffling one foot in front of the other they moved forward with the line.

    "Riiiillleey!" screeched an unseen voice through the crowd. The silver sequined top and big boot wearing girl who owned the voice budged up between them. "Oh my gosh, I'm so glad you're here! This season is gonna be the best."

    "I know! Scotty told me in study hall he's going to try and break the school record for double doubles," Riley said turning his back on Nora to talk to Kelsey.

    Nora seethed under the surface, but refused to give up

so easily. "My dad told me that college scouts are going to be at like every home game," she said and successfully regained Riley's attention.

"Really? That is so cool."

"How would he know?" Kelsey cut in.

"He's in sports promotion. It's pretty much his job to know," Nora answered.

"He! Maybe I should join the team!" Riley said miming a fade away jumper.

"Ohmigosh yes!" Kelsey squealed grabbing onto his bicep and turning him towards her again.

"Three students?" asked the attendant behind the ticket counter.

"Ah, no, make it two," Nora said and stepped out of line.

"What? Nora!" Riley called out after her as she walked away. "Hey, Hey!" he said and grabbed her sleeve. She stopped walking and turned to face him.

"We lost our spot in line."

"I am so annoyed that that is what you are choosing to say to me right now."

"What do you want me to say?" Riley snapped, annoyance filling his voice as well.

"I don't know."

"Nora," Riley said, taking her hand and for a second it felt like old times. Nora sniffed back a tear and squeezed his hand. The crowd continued to surge around them so Riley pulled Nora along the sidewalk out of the way.

"Why are you always walking away?" he asked her.

"I'm sorry. There is just so much going on. Sometimes I just need a break. And Kelsey doesn't ever improve a situation."

"What's wrong with Kelsey?"

"Are you kidding?"

"No," he paused, sighed and tipped her chin up with

his free hand so he could look into her eyes. "Nora, come on. Let's go have fun. You've been such a zombie since Flynn left."

"Left! Riley, it's not like she went on vacation! She could die down there! And so could my sister!"

"I know Nora-"

"You say that, but clearly you don't get it. I'm not sorry I've been a zombie… or not any fun," she went on, rage was blazing out of her eyes, a laser trained on Riley's unequipped face.

"Look, Nora. I'm not cut out for this."

"They maybe you should go."

"Really?" Riley asked, unsure if he felt wounded or relived. Nora saw the relief. For once she just wanted someone to have some answers. All Riley had were questions. She managed to choke out,

"Yes, go. Have fun." She spat the last word out as if it had four letters instead of its unsuspecting and simple three. He barely made it past the ticket counter before Kelsey pounced on him, extra ticket in hand. He looked back once to see if Nora had followed him, but she wouldn't know. She was already half way down the block.

Chapter 21
ARK

"It's always nice to dislike someone together." – from: <u>Little Blog on the Prairie</u> by Cathleen Davit Bell

    Flynn was holed up in the kitchen pantry again. As she talked to Nora her laughter and gasps and shrieks could be heard through the metal door. While the other members of the ARK found her sound effects more than mildly annoying, they put up with it because upon her exit of the pantry, Flynn emerged resembling a normal human being, instead of the empty shell of a person that usually walked around the ARK in her place.
    Tonight their topic of discussion was Kelsey.
    "I can't believe she stole clothes from Savannah's closet!" Flynn cried.
    "I can't believe I have to eat lunch with Simon everyday just to avoid her. But that's not even the worst part! You should see the way she flirts with Riley! Ugh. I just loooooathe her entirely!"
    "I hate her too and I've never even officially met her," Flynn said in support.
    "You've met her. Just not this version of her. It's like her mean girl qualities weren't able to fully blossom until she ascended the throne of popularity."
    "I'm sorry," Flynn commiserated. "She sounds absolutely awful."
    "She is," Nora sighed. "But it's better now that I have childishly gossiped about her with you."
    The girls talked and talked and talked while the power charge on the converter changed from green to yellow, and then from yellow to orange. When its battery light cast a red

glow on Flynn's face she told Nora she had to hang up. The power supply was super limited in the ARK and already Flynn feared the barrage of scolding remarks Caspian would undoubtedly give her about wasting their precious resources for useless chit chat.

"Talk tomorrow?" Nora asked hopefully.

"Probably not, better wait a couple days."

"Sooner if you can?"

"I promise."

Flynn pressed the end button and paused a moment to sadly inspect her less than perfect cuticles. After giving herself a brief pep-talk and putting on a brace face to present to her surely awaiting brother, she stood and opened the pantry door.

No pep-talk or brave face could have prepared her for the somber faces that swung her way when she slid out of the closet. Her exit had silenced the heated debate that began shortly after she'd left to talk to Nora. Now that the submarine was ready, who would go to the Outlier Station and who would stay behind? After another hour, after tempers had flared, after tears had been spilled, Professor Sorenson sent them all to bed like little children.

In the end, Anton's accusation rang true and the professors made the decision alone, long after the others had stopped tossing and turning in their sleeping bags and finally fallen asleep.

Chapter 22
ARK

"In the arithmetic of love, one plus one equals everything, and two minus one equals nothing." – anonymous

The professors' selections were revealed at breakfast the following morning.

Nina's parents hadn't signed her up for this. Well, they had, but not in the grand scope that the rest of the under-ager's parents had. She surely needed to be removed to what was presumed a safer environment. Noah, the youngest, was also a no-brainer decision.

Professor Sorenson refused to "abandon ship", so by default, Professor Bebee was the accompanying adult on the field trip. Caspian's senior status and Flynn's technical knowledge gave them roles that needed to be filled at the ARK, so they also stayed. The rest of the members and their abilities were debated and analyzed and eventually the final list was made. Professor Bebee, Nina, Noah, Sonora, Luke and Anton would be leaving for the Outlier Station shortly after breakfast.

Breakfast was eaten in stilted bursts of talk and silence, emotions thicker than the oatmeal they ate and definitely harder to swallow. Noah sat with Flynn unsure how to react. Pumped by the prospect of seeing his parents, but bummed at leaving the only home he'd ever known, he sat saying nothing. Flynn tried to distract him with a story involving the happiest place on earth and rollercoasters. Luke caught her eye and winked at her. It was comforting knowing someone else was thinking about how she was doing, but she wasn't sure she was accomplishing the same thing for Noah. It was, however, helping to distract herself from the other drama around her.

Caspian and Nina sat close together, communicating in sighs and sideways glances. For them the tragedy of leaving the ARK was momentarily overshadowed by the tragedy of leaving each other. Nina tried to view the situation as a mature adult, but kept caving into her teenage frame of mind. Caspian for once in his life could appreciate his sister's giftedness in the emotional quadrant of her brain.

Stillman sat with Sonora, passing along messages he'd like her to tell their parents if they were in fact at the Outlier Station. Anton, who'd been itching to escape for weeks, was positively bouncing off the walls.

Little was said and less was eaten, but the daily ritual helped add a hint of normalcy to the atmosphere. Following their typical schedule, the crew cleaned up after themselves and then sat back down to await their next instructions. Final preparations were completed including double checking the cargo list, a buoyancy check on the submarine and a last minute check of the scouting reports.

The sea turtles arrived at first light and dutifully allowed the ropes to be tied around their shells. Just as they were testing the knots 'Cuda swam frantically forward in search of Caspian. He quickly relayed the information from double agent Hale.

"When are they planning to attack?"

"We don't know."

"With a limited crew left at the ARK, I'm not sure we can do anything, but we can have Professor Bebee and everyone else in the submarine keep their eyes peeled for any suspicious activity," Caspian offered.

"What about the harpoon? Will the submarine support its added weight?" Luke asked after having overheard the conversation.

"I think it should," Caspian quickly calculated. "But you'd need to be outside of the submarine to fire it."

"That's fine. I volunteer," Luke said determinedly.

"Alright then, we're set," Caspian said looking back to 'Cuda.

"Thank you," 'Cuda said "Swim safe,"

"Swim strong," Caspian finished.

Together they stood to the side, a single pane of glass separating them as they watched the others load themselves and their gear into the submarine, which they had recently dubbed *Moses*. It wasn't the Red Sea they were crossing and seaweed wasn't exactly the same as reeds, but the connections were close enough. After a few minutes Caspian excused himself from 'Cuda to say some goodbyes. He hugged his little brother and reminded him to tell their parents that Flynn was back in the ARK and that everyone was doing the best they could to fix the situation.

As Luke stepped forward to climb in *Moses* Flynn grabbed his forearm and pulled him aside.

"I understand why Caspian and I aren't going, but I'm not happy that Noah is traveling without either of us. I realize I'm asking you for a lot of promises lately," here she paused while a blush crept up her face thinking about their recent conversations. "but please, promise me you'll watch out for Noah."

"Of course," Luke answered.

"And if you have any time left over-"

"Good lord Flynn! I doubt Hera was this high maintenance!" Luke interrupted.

"I was just going to say, watch out for yourself too." She stood up on tiptoe, kissed him on his pale cheek and disappeared around the corner. Luke rubbed his face absentmindedly, smiled and then returned to the submarine to load up.

Sonora and Nina stood inside the transparent shell of the submarine holding hands. A jumble of emotions mixed inside them, an unidentifiable cocktail of apprehension, fear and hope. When Caspian ducked his head inside and softly kissed Nina on the top of her head, her emotions brimmed over and she threw herself into his arms. Tears streamed openly down her face.

"Don't be afraid. The professors will take care of us. A month from now this will all just be a bad dream," he whispered in her ear. She nodded in reply, unable to form discernable words. A final squeeze and she returned to her spot, too embarrassed to make eye contact with anyone inside the vessel.

"Text me when you get there!" Pac kidded as he sealed them in. "No, for real. Let us know when you get there."

"Will do bro," Luke responded with a thumbs up.

Thanks to Flynn and Luke, fronds of seaweed covered every available surface of the submarine. Except for a small window at the very front of the floating box, the passengers sat blind. It's a shame the situation was clouded with so much stress; it would have been a very relaxing way to travel.

Shortly after leaving the ARK, the sea turtles halted their forward movement and ducked behind the seaweed, hidden from view. Should they need to duck and cover, this maneuver would hopefully do the trick. A regiment of security accompanied the travel party and confirmed the safety measure's success before swimming ahead to scout for any enemies in their path.

The sea turtle's speed with their cumbersome load was slow, but as one would expect from a turtle, progress was steady. Inside the submarine the crew nervously tracked their forward movement on a GPS and prayed to Poseidon for a safe arrival.

Chapter 23
Surface

"Sometimes love is a white flag. Sometimes love is standing tall. Sometimes love is a feather. Sometimes a cannon ball." – from: Love is War *by American Young*

Nora had stayed up late watching reruns of *L.A. Living*. With their conversation fresh in her mind, it was easy for Nora to pretend Flynn was on the other side of the couch, just as greedily mowing through a bowl of popcorn. When Nora's phone buzzed her awake the next morning she was surprised to see the screen show it was past ten o'clock. She had three new text messages and two more buzzed in as she swiped the screen to unlock it. The messages were from Riley. Her heart fluttered as she opened them, and then it immediately sank.

Riley: I can't do this anymore.

Riley: I think we should break up.

Riley: Neither of us make each other happy anymore and I don't know how to fix it.

Riley: I really did love you Nora, but it's over.

Riley: Please don't hate me.

Nora let the phone slide from her fingers and land with a thud on the beige carpeted floor. She pulled her covers up around her chin, buried her face into her pillow and cried. She knew that she didn't want to be with someone who didn't want to be with her, but it still hurt. She felt abandoned in her time of need and rejected by someone who used to find every single bit of her desirable. When she stopped crying a half hour later she picked up her phone and texted Riley back.

    Nora: Got it. Don't hate you. But don't want to talk to you right now either.

To Riley's credit he replied a minute later.

Riley: K. I understand.

Eleven o'clock came and went. Curiosity and hunger forced her to drag herself out of bed, into some sweats and downstairs to investigate why she'd been allowed to sleep so late, especially on a school day. A note was taped to the kitchen TV screen where Nora would be sure to see it.

Nora,
*   Dad has a trade show/conference in Tampa. I decided to go with him and stay overnight. We'll be home tomorrow before dinner. Call us if you need anything.*
*   Love,*
*   Mom*

Beneath the note was $20 for takeout. Nora battled feelings of gratefulness for being able to wallow in her self-pity and the increasing feeling of abandonment. If Luke hadn't laid down next to her on the couch while she ate cereal and watched awful day-time talk shows, she might have completely fallen to pieces.

Chapter 24
Waters near the Outlier Station

"Honor is like an island rugged and without a beach; once we have left it, we can never return." – Nicholas Boileau Despreaux

"We're too late," Nina said sadly.

The sight and stench of the massacred swordfish littered the scene. Carcasses. Everywhere they looked there were the remains of swordfish bodies. Bits and pieces left over after the battle that had previously ensued were all that remained. No words formed in their throats for a long time. Finally Sonora spoke.

"How could they do this? What good could possibly come from slaughtering another creature?" she choked out between sobs.

"You forget that they don't care about good," Professor Bebee gently reminded her, as she placed a comforting arm around her shaking shoulders.

"They don't care about anything," Luke said disgusted.

"Not quite right Luke. They don't care about right and wrong or good and bad or even the repercussions of their actions. But they do care about their supremacy," Professor Bebee.

"What do we do?" Nina asked.

"We make the best of the situation," Professor Bebee instructed.

Following Professor Bebee's directions the turtles dropped their reigns connected to Moses, and set to work. As the turtles gathered and stored the swordfish meat, Luke stood guard, the harpoon resting on his shoulder. A few scouts created a perimeter of protection as well. The swordfishes' bodily sacrifice would feed the cause, literally.

An altar of sorts was erected of stones and any inedible swordfish remains. As they watched the sad affair they struggled to comprehend what their eyes saw. Questions swirled in their brains. When the alter was complete each person inside the sub offered a genuine prostration of gratitude and respect and made silent promises to put an end to these crazy days.

On his way back to the sub Luke paused at a mound of sand.

"Look at this," Luke said scuffing the edge of it with his fin, flipping the sand off to expose a mass of purplish flesh.

"A tentacle. Make sure not to touch it. It can extremely dangerous even in its severed state," instructed Professor Bebee from within the sub. "Quite perplexing."

"The dolphins must be widening their circle of prey," Nina chanced.

"I doubt it. The owner of that tentacle, be it a squid or an octopus, is known to eat dolphins. This one definitely could," Sonora explained. "It's so large."

"The color of it almost matches that rock back there," Nina pointed out.

"You're right," Sonora agreed. "But do you think that means it was a predator or prey?"

"Good questions," Professor Bebee "But right now I think Luke should get back into the sub and we should continue on our way." Following their teacher's instructions, Luke got back into the submarine and removed his wet gear.

Luke looked around one more time at the devastating scene. "I don't feel like this is enough," he said, toweling off his shaggy hair. "How does a few thank you's and a pile of rocks make this okay?

"It's not okay," said Nina staring out the window. "But it's not over either."

Chapter 25
Surface

"Happy is a huge river right now and I've forgotten how to swim."
– from: The Crossover by Alexander Kwame

If it weren't for a World History exam, she would have scrapped the rest of her school day and stayed perfectly planted on the couch. But using her better judgment, she showered, pulled on something comfy, yet cute, and headed out the door.

Nora spent a portion of her long walk to school mentally reviewing the material for her test. But the majority of her walk was spent strategizing how to avoid a public run in with Riley. She wasn't ready for that yet. Selecting a side door, Nora entered the school, checked in at the office and then made a bee-line for the back row of her history class. The bell rang, attendance was taken and the access code to the online test was given. Thirty-seven minutes later Nora clicked submit and her test results flashed in a failing red across the screen. Maybe it would have been better to stay home.

The final bell of the day rang and released the weekend ready teenagers to the hallway. They spilled out of the doors, onto the sidewalks and into the world beyond the walls of Bay City High School. Dreading another long walk, Nora turned to the open locker next to her and said,

"Hey Brittany, do you think you could drop me off at the Smoothie Shak on your way home?"

"On Nora!" Brittany began brightly. "You mean now that Flynn has left and Riley's dumped you, you want to be friends again?" She slammed her locker shut, and without waiting for an answer continued, "That's not really how it works."

Nora blinked back tears, shut her own locker and left the building. Fearing another horrible verbal beating she walked away from the high school, head down, not wanting to even chance making eye contact with anyone. Nora was as surprised as the bored afternoon waitress when the bell above the PitStop door jingled. She hadn't meant to come here, but it's where she ended up. Her eyes scanned the small restaurant looking for Simon's dorky hat and when she found the place completely empty sat down in a booth anyway. Pulling the twenty dollar bill from her pocket she ordered a basket of fries and a chocolate malt. Thirty minutes and fifteen hundred calories later she was still the only one in the restaurant. She couldn't put off the Smoothie Shak any longer, especially if she didn't want to be late. Nora stood, waved weakly to the waitress and started her walk across town.

Chapter 26
ARK

"All you need is the plan, the road map and the courage to press onto your destination," – Earl Nightengale

The one mile journey seemed to have taken an eternity, but finally they had arrived. As the subtle glow of interior lights flooded out across the ocean floor the subdued passengers of the submarine came to life. Forgetting for a minute the troubles stacked against them, their hope surged. Noah wiped a sleeve across his eyes, attempting to hide his tears of relief from the others. When the sea turtles stopped 200 yards away and dropped their towing formation to hide, their momentary joy was replaced by panic.

"What is happening?" Professor Bebee whispered, her face pressed to their small window.

"The scouts have seen a group of Water Warriors headed this way," Kurma informed through the miniscule windshield. "We don't want to risk being caught or worse. Extinguish any light creating device inside and keep quiet. Hopefully they will pass soon."

The scene inside reminded Nina of a severe weather drill at school. Everyone sat quietly, knees balled up to their chests, ears listening for any clue as to what was going on in the world they could not see. Professor Bebee held Sonora's hand and Luke crouched next to Noah, one arm protectively around his shoulders and the other resting on the harpoon. Anton struck a soldierly pose, bluffing a faux fearlessness that they all could see straight through. Nina's hands shook so she tucked them under her armpits and focused on calm breathing.

Unseen to the crew, the troops militantly swam

through the water. They moved as a mass, a herd, in perfect rows. Although no external markings were present, it was easy to discern who was in charge. The commanders' black beady eyes focused straight ahead as if telepathically guiding the troops forward. The sudden stop of movement caused the seaweed to sway back and forth, offering brief and terrifying views to those huddled inside the submarine. When Adonis' now familiar voice began speaking, they clapped their hands over their mouths to keep their fear from escaping verbally.

"Our next move is to commandeer the supply of changing solution. We will then carefully transport it to the coastal city the land walkers call: "New Orleans"." No one dared question him. Whether their brains were incapable of debate or the attack on the swordfish too recent, the warriors continued to listen on in silence. Adonis paused, searching the faces of his army, checking to see that they were on board, rabid with hate for the humans. Mostly he sensed fear, but fear meant compliance and so he continued, "My scouts have informed me that the change has not traveled that distance by current. They remain ignorant creatures still. I, Adonis, with the changing solution will enlighten them. And in doing so, I will convince them to join our cause, avoid the fishing nets and therefore starve the land walkers." The troops remained still, but a few began to beat their new swords upon their scales, a low rumbling soundtrack to accompany Adonis' tirade. "We will repeat this again and again and again. In Anchorage, Reykjavik, Tokyo, Rio de Janiero, and Cape Town! Alexandria, Istanbul, Perth, and Melbourne!" Adonis was now shouting to be heard over the roar of his troops. "We will give the gift of knowledge and speech and then starve the humans until they beg us to stop. But will we stop?"

Their reply was deafening. Armor clanging, cheers echoing, clicks and squeals and shouts mingling to create a giant wave of noise that crashed down around the submarine. Nina wasn't the only one shielding her head and ears from the assaulting noise. Noah was no longer hiding his tears of utter terror, so different from the happy tears that a minute earlier had run down his round face. At some unseen signal, the noise was cut off and an eerie silence followed.

"And then, when their children are starving, and the mothers are begging for food, we'll graciously comply… with poisoned fare. Renegades, prisoners, deserters, any against us, we'll gather them up, poison them and serve them on a pretty platter. Come! Toward a future free from human destruction, toward a future where we make the rules, toward a future where you'll be free!"

The troops cheered again, this time in a controlled measure, as they began moving again, away from the submarine. Commander Hale had heard enough. Double agent or not, he needed to leave… to report back to 'Cuda, to keep his head intact and his body toxin free. He edged to the side of the moving columns and then pulled out of rank, appearing to inspect their forward movement. As his troops passed a section of reef he hung back, then darted to a small cove and immediately found a space similar to his own coloring. He slowly let his miniature swordfish armor sink to the floor. Hale stilled his racing heart and kept his rarely blinking eyes transfixed in a solitary location. Minimizing movement of all kind, he melted into the coral scenery, virtually disappearing.

Chapter 27
Outlier Station

"When you're frightened, don't sit still. Keep on doing something. The act of doing will give you back your courage." – George Ogot

Wrapped in the arms of his mother, Noah felt safe. He felt protected. And once his terror subsided and he heard the story again, he began to feel angry… and brave.

After the Water Warriors had left, the sea turtles waited for their scouts to return and announce the way was clear. Picking up the ropes and pulling, they made the final trek to the Outlier Station faster than anyone would have believed possible.

Inside the Outlier Station mass hysteria had ensued as the scientists saw their visitors delayed amidst the middle of the Water Warriors. Trapped helplessly without sufficient weaponry or vehicle to retrieve them, they watched in breathless anticipation. By the time Adonis and his army had moved on, the loading dock was ready to receive them. An avalanche of emotions, hugs, words and tears cascaded into the station with the children and Professor Bebee.

"Alright, alright. Enough. We have work to do," Professor Bebee shouted out. The hugging and emoting came to an abrupt end. "Terrible as it seems, it is far worse than you know." As fast as humanly possible, the petite and fiery woman told their tale.

"So the ARK is in shambles, the PE-328 is a complete bust and no one on the surface is doing anything about it," Anton's father angrily recapped.

"Pretty much," Anton agreed, an exaggerated look of annoyance on his face.

"Well, what was that out there? Could you hear what

that maniac was saying?" another parent asked.

"Sounded an awful lot like a pep talk," Luke said. "Like Adonis needed them big time fired up."

"For what?" Mrs. Brinestone asked.

"To steal the PE-328. They are going to change all of the creatures and then convince them to turn against us, by refusing to be food," Sonora supplied.

"Do they know where the PE-328 solution is?" Mr. Perone asked, directing the question to his son, Anton.

"If there's one thing we've learned through this, they aren't dumb. They have plans. And anyway it wouldn't take a genius to figure out where it came from," Anton said.

"So you think they are headed to the ARK now?" Sonora's mother asked as she clutched her daughter close, the horror of her imagination flashing across her face.

"That's why we have work to do," Professor Bebee said sternly. "No time for talk, we must go back and get the others. We must leave now."

It took 12 minutes to decide who would return and who would stay. The submarine could only carry a limited amount of weight, so most everyone would need to remain behind in order to make room for those left in the ARK to make the return trip. Fin-fresh turtles showed up soon after the decision was made. The submarine was unpacked of anything carrying a significant amount of weight, except the harpoon; that item stayed safely stowed inside. Goodbyes were intense and brief and a half an hour after arriving at the Outlier Station, *Moses*, carrying Mr. Brinestone and Luke, was gone.

**Chapter 28
Surface**

"The heart breaks quietly. No one can hear it." – from: *Nine Days a Queen* by Ann Rinaldi

It had been a pretty awful day, but the worst part came during her shift at the Smoothie Shak. As Nora stood mixing ingredients for a protein packed power shake she heard the warning sign things were about to get worse. The high pitched squeal - part laugh, part torture device - could only belong to one person. Nora's gut wrenched inside her and then turned completely inside out when she saw Kelsey draped all over Riley. Her knees buckled out from beneath her and she crumpled to the pavement. The over muscled, too-tiny-tank-top-wearing customer leaned over the counter to check on her. She waved him off, refusing the money in his hand and whispered up to him "It's on the house." Confused, he accepted his good fortune and lumbered off.

Nora took a deep breath and peeked over the edge of the counter and saw them. Kelsey and Riley walked hand in hand down the boardwalk toward the edge of the pier. They paused to look out at the waves and Kelsey ran her hair through Riley's god like golden hair, hair Nora used to love. As if this wasn't torture enough, he leaned in and kissed her.

Too much. It was too much. Nora turned and vomited into the closest receptacle she could find, which unfortunately was a smoothie blender. How many times should a girl have to pick herself up in one day? Wiping her mouth on the back of her Hawaiian shirt sleeve Nora stood up and was face to face with Riley... and Kelsey.

"We're closed," Nora blurted.

"No we're not!" an angry voice boomed behind her.

"Could my day get any worse?" Nora mumbled.

Nora's manager brushed her aside as he shouldered his way into the tiki hut that was really only built to house one employee at a time.

"How can I help you?" the manager asked.

"I'll take a strawberry banana bomber," Kelsey ordered, eyes trained on Nora's desperate face.

"And for you?"

"Nah, I'm good," Riley managed to croak out, at which Kelsey rolled her eyes and pouted her lips.

"Aright, one strawberry banana bomber coming up," the manager said and reached for the nearest blender.

"Oh! Don't-" Nora winced, "use that one," Nora finished as four pairs of eyes stared horrified at the pre-chewed fries floating in half digested milkshake.

"You can go," the manager said through tightly clenched teeth. "Leave your keys and name tag."

Nora slid the keys out of her pocket and placed them on the counter. When her name tag stayed stubbornly stuck to her god-awful shirt she ripped it clean off and placed it next to the keys. Without making eye contact she said, "I'm so sorry."

"Just go," the manager said coldly, and then turning back to his customers, "I am so sorry about that. How about free smoothies for life?"

"Oh! Yes please!" Kelsey squealed.

There was nothing left for Nora to do but walk away. But where? She had nowhere to go and no one to see.

Chapter 29
Outlier Station

"Fate is like a strange unpopular restaurant filled with odd little waiters who bring you things you never asked for and don't always like." – Lemony Snicket

"I can't believe I'm saying this, but I actually think she'd have been safer up there on the surface with who knows how many teenage hooligans," Mrs. Brinestone nagged when Noah told her of Flynn's return to the ARK. "Oh well, nothing I can do about it now I suppose. Don't you kids know you're supposed to check with your parents before making life altering decisions?"

"Hey, don't shoot me!" Noah said, throwing his hands up in mock surrender. "I'm just the messenger."

"I won't. As long as you let me hug you one more time." Noah settled down next to her where she sat on the couch.

The Outlier Station, while built by the same scientists, had a completely different atmosphere that the ARK. Built in a retreat mindset, the furniture was overstuffed and super comfy and as the reunited families sat together, they could almost forget their current ordeal.

"Now that we've told you everything about the ARK why don't you tell us what the heck you've been doing?" Noah said accusingly. "Why didn't you come back?"

In a calm voice Mrs. Brinestone relayed their near month long nightmare. After releasing the PE-328 in a variety of strategic locations, they lingered to watch the results. When the results were not instantly visible, they decided to take a break and refill their oxygen tanks at the Outlier Station since it would be faster than swimming the mile back to the ARK.

Everything was going fine until they tried to leave. Blocking the main exit was a large pod of dolphins. Excited at first at the rare scene, the scientists rushed out to greet the usually playful creatures. But before the scientists could even place a flipper clad foot in the water the dolphins charged and aggressively forced them back inside.

For a while it was a cat and mouse chase between the two Outlier Station exits. Just as the scientists decided to make a break for it and push their way through the disgruntled dolphins, the sharks showed up.

Resigned to staying put, at least for the moment, the scientists sat, as they sat now, in the makeshift living room. Three days passed. Every attempted escape was thwarted. They began to sleep in shifts, conserve food, monitor the animal behavior and filter mass quantities of fresh drinking water.

On the evening of the third day, just before last light, Adonis paid them a visit. He explained his plan of hostile takeover and told the scientists that if they interfered in anyway, their children – not them – would be the ones held accountable. When the daily arrivals of animal carcasses started arriving, they knew enough not to test Adonis' word.

"Why didn't you try to contact us?" Sonora asked at one point in the story.

"We tried several times that first night, and no one answered our converter calls. By the next morning, the communication signals were completely scrambled and all we heard was static. Savannah tried to get through to the surface a few times on her cell phone, but it was too water logged to do anything more than spastically vibrate a for a few seconds before turning off."

The children turned to look where Mrs. Brinestone gestured, and they saw for the first time, a disheveled form, huddling in blankets next to the window. This was the spot Savannah had first selected upon arriving at the Outlier

Station, choosing to distance herself both physically and mentally from the "psycho scientists" as she called them in her head. *It's like they don't even speak English. And seriously those clothes? You've got to be kidding me. Talk about social suicide.* She was willing to put up with the cold that poured off the glass and in her positive moments, however fleeting they might be, she was able to enjoy the beautiful landscapes as the sun filtered down from the surface. But as night fell to the ocean floor, the shadows came, and with them, Savannah's fear grew.

    For a while she moved to the middle of the room. Observational by nature, the scientists took immediate notice, but recognizing their newcomer harbored many of Flynn's strange female teenage ways, refrained from commenting. Savannah camped out on a couch for hours huddled beneath a blanket. But the fear of the unknown won out and before the day was done, she returned to her perch next to the window. During the day she dozed in and out of sleep, but as the water darkened her anxiety grew. Through the long hours of the ocean's dark night she sat propped up waiting and watching for the monster she was sure would come and smash the self-deemed fragile walls of her prison, sending her to a watery grave.

    Savannah knew there was nothing she could do to stop an attack or save herself if one did occur, but the watching calmed her and gave her something to do. Completely obsessed with her own fear and devoid of any positive distraction, she let fear overwhelm her. Dark circles started to form under her eyes. She refused to leave the window to do anything but go to the bathroom. What little food she did consume, she ate on the window ledge that had become her permanent post.

    The mothers took turns sitting with her from time to time, offering her, some comfort of company. At first they asked her questions… about her life, her friends, the surface celebrities Flynn idolized, movies, shopping… but when she refused to even look away from the window, they turned their questions into a constant stream of chatter about the creatures that passed by her window. Watching her visibly relax as each harmless creature passed by and was described was payment enough. They only wished someone was there to comfort their own sons and daughters a mile away.

Since the children had arrived, Savannah had been watching the group sullenly from the corner. In her opinion the whole situation clearly sucked and she didn't see how the arrival of the mini-scientists made it any better. Now on top of being bored and paranoid, she added perpetual annoyance and socially awkward situations to her ever growing gripe list. Nina didn't look a thing like Nora, but Savannah was sure she carried at least a few of Nora's traits.

"How did you get here?" Stillman asked.

"Those crazy dolphins dragged me here, to this black hole." Savannah answered in an abbreviated version of the story.

"She's lucky to be alive," Mrs. Brinestone added.

"That's a matter of opinion," Savannah said with false bravado and then turned her back on the crowded room to stare out of the window.

"Wait!" Anton shouted suddenly, "Where's Carl?"

"What do you mean, 'where's Carl'?" Mrs. Grier spoke up.

"Isn't he back at the ARK?" Mr. Grier added his panicked voice to the conversation. The children looked around the room, their helpless faces searching for an answer that couldn't be found.

"There was an accident," Professor Bebee began. Mrs. Grier both melted to the floor and shrieked hysterically. Her husband bent to comfort her, shushing both to soothe and to hear the details of his son's demise.

Hours later the Outlier Station was silent as a tomb. Mr.

and Mrs. Grier had retreated to a private corner to grieve and wonder, cry and question, hope and pray. The rest of the crew's sleeping bodies littered the floor, draped across chairs and couches. Noah lay curled up in his mother's lap, while she leaned against the wall keeping watch and worrying about the rest of her family and crew. All was not well. All was not at peace. But all was quiet, and for now, that was enough.

Chapter 30
ARK

"Patience is the ability to idle your motor when you feel like stripping your gears." – Barbara Johnson

The battering ram pounded into the fiberglass window. The sound reverberated through the entire ARK. Boom. Boom. Boom. Tiny spiderwebs of cracks were visible in the domed ceiling covering the aqua farm. It would not hold much longer. Boom. Boom. Boom.

Pac, who had been sent to investigate the sound raced back to the kitchen to report. The panic on his face and in his voice halted any questions before they were even formed on their lips. Instantly mobile, the crew grabbed their packs and scanned the room for any items they deemed useful in their hasty retreat.

An ear splitting crash and sudden change of air pressure let them know the enemy's attempt had succeeded. The crew stopped their frantic search and focused every fiber of their being on moving forward. Professor Sorenson's bulky body was falling behind, unable to fly through the hallways as fast as the youth who fled in front of him. He was the last to reach the loading dock and once he slumped into the room, Stillman and Pac sealed the door shut behind him and engaged the room's own air pressure regulating system.

"The only way out is up!" Stillman shrieked near hysterics. Already outside the ARK the Water Warriors were gathering, crowding the only remaining exit, their hunger and bloodlust written clearly on their faces.

"How? There is no passenger compartment anymore. We took it out to build Moses. And even if there was, we wouldn't have enough energy to power it," Pac thought aloud. "We'll have to climb out. Can we rig up a cargo net, or ladder or something?"

"That will only work if we have someone from the top, anchoring the ropes as we climb," Flynn said, troubleshooting as usual.

"What time is it? Will anyone be at the station?" Stillman asked.

"It's hours past dinner time. Most likely they've all gone home, but we can try," Professor Sorenson said beginning to recover from their mad dash.

Huddled at the entrance of the TUBE the crew stood and screamed and hollered and banged on the fiberglass walls. The sound traveled up the TUBE and into the station and echoed around its empty rooms. Three straight minutes of screaming produced no results. Pac leaned back against the transparent wall and rest his head against it before sliding down to sit on the floor. The others followed suit. As they sat in the silence it was hard not to think that the quiet was an omen of their helpless future.

"We have twelve hours-worth of energy and oxygen in this room," Professor Sorenson said breaking the silence. "Unless water starts seeping through that door, we are safe… for now." He had hoped to calm them, make them feel better, but it wasn't working. "We can try to attract the attention of the Surface Station scientists again in the morning."

"Well what do we do now?" Flynn asked.

"We wait," Professor Sorenson answered.

Chapter 31
Surface

"My honey I know with the dawn that you will be gone. But tonight, you belong to me." – Gene Austin

    Alex found her sitting atop her Hawaiian print shirt in the sand. Her shoulders were a slightly shaking silhouette against the setting sun. Alex took off his sweatshirt and draped it around her shoulders before sitting down next to her. For a long time neither one spoke. Eventually Nora stopped crying and realized that Alex was holding her hand. It felt nice to have someone acknowledge her existence, even better that it was in a comforting and judgment-free way.

    "Bad day?" Alex asked.

    "Ahahha," Nora laughed bitterly swiping the tears and unattractive snot away from her face with the back of her free hand. "I wouldn't even know where to start describing how completely awful today was. Which is fine, because I don't want to relive a second of it. Even if it means getting your pity."

    "It wouldn't be pity. I just want you to stop feeling this way," Alex said and gave a quick squeeze to her hand. "I want you to be happy."

    "Happy? Is that all?" Nora asked, contemplating if such a thing was possible.

    "Well, I'd like a happy you, but I'll settle for any version of you I can get."

    "Oh Alex," Nora said leaning into this shoulder. "Please don't. I don't know if I have the energy to tell you no."

    "Then don't," he said cupping her chin in his hand and turning her face towards his. He stared into her tear-filled eyes, leaned in and kissed her. Nora pulled back.

"You know this is as close to forbidden as two people in modern society can get right?" Nora asked.

"Yes, but it doesn't make me want to kiss you any less."

"I know," Nora said and sighed.

"I know we'll have to tell them," Alex sighed, shifting so that his forehead rested on Nora's and so that his eyes lined up directly with hers.

"I know." Nora closed her eyes and let Alex kiss her. Her heart screamed at her guilty conscience, but the day had been too much. Her parents had ditched her, Riley had dumped her and Flynn was gone. Alex however, was here. He was always here. They kissed and kissed and kissed some more. For Nora an intangible need was quenched by a tangible means and these moments of oblivion overshadowed the terrors of the day. Suddenly tasting salt, Alex stopped kissing Nora and again held her face tenderly in his hands.

"Okay," he said. "Enough for now."

"Thank you for saving me," Nora sobbed. "Tonight, this week, this whole mess. Thank you for always being here for me."

"I know it will be hard for you to decide who you love more, me or Flynn," Alex whispered in her ear as she cried on his shoulder. "But I want you to know, I pick you."

Chapter 32
ARK

"We cross bridges as we come to them and burn them behind us, with nothing to show for our progress except a memory of the smell of smoke and presumption that once our eyes watered." – from: Rozencratz and Guildenstern Are Dead by Tom Stoppard

A piercing light cut through the night black water and startled the dozing members of the slowly flooding ARK.

"What is that?" asked Flynn, rubbing her bleary eyes.

"It's *Moses*! They're back!" Caspian shouted. Instantly the crew was on their feet, pressing to the window to see.

"They'll never get through the Water Warriors!" Stillman worried.

It was true, the submarine had stalled several yards from the loading dock, looking for the best way to break through the wall of fishy flesh before them. The turtles tread nervously, eyeing their enemies poised to attack. Suddenly the warriors began to twitch and wiggle. A few broke rank and backed out of their position.

"What in Posideon's realm?" Pac exclaimed.

"Are they afraid of Moses?" Stillman asked, curious about the animals' strange behavior.

"No," Pac answered and pointed up. "But they are afraid of those guys."

A cloud of jellyfish descended on the scene, ensnaring and devouring any creature it encountered. Their pink flesh enveloped and ingested predator after predator. No matter how loudly or fiercely the commanders screamed for the Water Warriors to hold their positions, they fled. Pandemonium spread through the ranks and a flurry of scales and fins and swords flashed in front of the crew.

It took only minutes for the jellyfish to displace and replace the Water Warriors. Their undulating forms floated serenely, protecting the remaining structure of the ARK and the crew within it. As *Moses* approached, the jellyfish peeled away enough to let the submarine travel to the ARK and safely dock.

Pac and Stillman hefted the door of the submarine open to reveal Mr. Brinestone and Luke, their heads popping almost comically out of Moses like prairie dogs. Remaining in the ARK was clearly not an option and so the crew quickly piled in, a tide of gratitude and emotion. The door was sealed and the crew took seats, ready to sail safe and away.

As the crew faced forward, mentally preparing for departure, the submarine slowly sunk. As it bumped along the ocean floor, it sent up clouds of silt.

"We're too heavy," Luke said, the devastation in his voice almost painful to hear.

"What can we remove?" Flynn asked.

"There's nothing left," Dr. Brinestone said in a hollow voice. "We removed it all before we left the Outlier Station."

"Then what do we do?" Stillman asked in horror.

"I'll stay," Professor Sorenson said, standing and making his way to the exit.

"No!" Flynn gasped. "I mean, what'll you do?"

"I don't know, but a captain goes down with his ship. I will not leave any of you to carry my burden." Already the big man was climbing the ladder to leave. As he found solid footing on the loading dock, the submarine slowly rose off the ocean floor. A sad smile of satisfaction spread across the professor's face.

"We'll come back," Flynn promised.

"Don't. It isn't safe. Who knows how long Moses will hold up? It wasn't meant for multiple heavy trips. Don't worry, with only one person breathing in here, the oxygen supply will last much longer." When Flynn didn't look convinced he continued earnestly, "I'll find a way out. This big old brain still has some juice in it yet," the professor said and pointed to his head full of unruly white hair. Putting on a brave face he sealed the door shut and waved them off. With the help of the sea turtles, the submarine moved forward leaving the professor and the ARK behind. Before heading back to the Outlier Station they paused at the front of the jellyfish wall of protection and surveyed the scene.

Through the observation window they could see a battle rage behind the glass. Barracudas, sea snakes, and angelfish battled the Water Warriors, forcing them back out into the open ocean where they were quickly surrounded, stung and devoured by the jellyfish. They knew they should leave, that the rest of their crew remain at the Outlier Station waiting, but they couldn't tear their eyes away.

The magnificent bubble that had been their home for more than a decade was almost completely flooded, the water level clearly visible through the observation window. Water cascaded down stair cases and splashed through grated walk ways. While most of the furniture remained bolted to the floor, various chairs and assorted pieces of lab equipment floated haphazardly.

"I'm upset we had to leave him behind, but I'm glad the professor isn't here to see this," Dr. Brinestone said sadly. Almost as if signifying its death, the lights of the ARK flickered and went out, only to be shortly replaced by a bioluminescent glow from within.

"The professor should still have a few hours left. The best we can hope for is the Surface Station to come to his aid," Dr. Brinestone said, if possible with even more sadness in his voice than moments before. "Come on. It's time to go."

Dr. Brinestone signaled Kurma and the turtles once again took up their reigns and began to pull the submarine away from the ARK. As they were maneuvering an about face Stillman shouted, "Stop!" As Moses came to a halt Jett worked his way up to their window.

"The perimeter of the ARK is secure and we will keep it that way," the jellyfish said by way of greeting.

"I can confirm this is true for the inside as well," 'Cuda said joining the impromptu war conference. "The ARK is fully under allied control."

"If it can no longer be our home, we are glad you can occupy it now. We'll tell the turtles they can use any pocketed airspace trapped in the ARK as their safe breathing space. Please welcome them when they return," Caspian communicated. "Swim safe friends, swim strong."

"I will, and I'm not afraid," Jett said moving to take up his security position outside of the ARK. "I mean, I might be if I had blood, or a brain, but since I have neither, I'm not afraid."

"I will tell Sonora the ARK is safe with your bloodless body in the front row of the infantry." Stillman said, trying to mimic his courageous friend's bravery.

"Maybe don't tell her I'm in the front row. She might worry," Jett said.

"Row three sound good?" Stillman wagered.

"Perfect. Swim safe, swim strong Stillman."

"You too Jett. Hopefully see you soon." Stillman watched as Jett joined his fellow jellyfish. He thought about how sad he would be to never see the jellyfish again and hoped that when all was said and done, this wasn't their final goodbye.

Ignoring Luke's advice, Caspian looked back at the ARK. Unlike Lot's wife, he did not turn to salt (or sea salt in this specific case). As he looked back at what had been his home for so long, he felt traitorous. He felt a margin better that they were not abandoning it to the Water Warriors, but instead leaving it in the fins of the ARK Allies who had come to their aid and rescue. Blinking away tears in his eyes, ignoring the clenching feeling in his chest, Caspian faced forward. Suddenly out in the open ocean he felt small and helpless.

Chapter 33
Underwater Cave

"It is impossible to live without failing at something, unless you live so cautiously that you might as well not have lived at all – in which case you have failed by default." – J.K. Rowling

The mission to capture the changing solution was a complete and total failure. Adonis knew it and the commanders knew it. What the commanders didn't know was how Adonis would react.

After their formation completely collapsed at the ARK, the commanders and Water Warriors alike scattered across open seawater. By a lucky chance a school of angelfish soldiers swam past Hale in his hidden coral cove. He gathered them up and together they remained hidden while they decided what to do next. Sensing they were on the losing side, the threadfin and grouper hightailed it as far away from the action as possible. The threat of poison further from their minds than Adonis' immediate disappointment and rage, they chose what they supposed to be the lesser of two evils.

Only the dolphins, Mahi, tuna and mackerels returned to Adonis' cave headquarters. They arrived in small regiments, checking in with their commanders as they arrived. They whispered in pockets around the cavern.

Where was Adonis? Had anyone spoken to him? How mad was he? Had he died in battle?

He kept them waiting almost two hours. When he entered the room it was not from the cavern's entrance as they expected, but instead he emerged from the catacombs of the cave. He swam in silently, his face a mask, empty of expression. The eerie calm was more worrisome than his typical temper and as he worked his way to his usual position at the front of the assembly, the Water Warriors shrank back from him, their fear momentarily overshadowing their loyalty. Finally he spoke to them, the icy chill in his voice freezing their focus on him alone.

"We must not be deterred. Yes, the humans have escaped. The bubble has been taken over by traitorous creatures and the changing solution remains inside. But this is not over. They have won the battle, but not the war." Adonis spoke softly, almost to himself, so different from his usual charismatic speech. But he was slowly regaining his momentum. He began to lock eyes with those few fearless commanders positioned nearby, pulling them back into his cause. "We have two options. We can attack the bubble again, swim in and take the changing solution for ourselves, or we can force the humans to make us a new batch. We know where the human children are. No doubt they swam away to their parents, but without a food supply to sustain their survival, we'll be able to easily sway them into giving us what we need."

The commanders began to nod in agreement and the warriors soon followed suit. Seeing their compliance put Adonis at ease and he began to return to his normal prime form.

"We will succeed. We will expand our regime and we will over throw the land-walkers." To this statement the Water Warriors cheered. Once again Adonis' army was ready. But ready for what? A new plan must be made, one that was fool proof, traitor proof, fail proof.

Adonis beckoned Admiral Marianus forward and then motioned for him to follow into the catacombs. Marianus cast a nervous glance back at the commanders and warriors, but they were already deep in conversations of their own – sharing battle stories, scars and heroic deeds gone unseen to anyone else. Their fear had been momentarily thawed and concern for Adonis' immediate whereabouts melted away.

They didn't see Adonis and Marianus slip into one of the countless tunnels and disappear into the catacombs.

When they emerged from the dark recesses of the cave several hours later the warriors were sleeping. Their peaceful breathing created mini streams of bubbles that floated up to the cave ceiling and gathered in a blanket of foam, gently swaying with the current above them.

Marianus swam straight past the cavern full of snoring soldiers who now refused to sleep in the catacombs, past the entrance guards and out of the cave with a single mission on his mind. Tonight he alone would turn the tables when he infiltrated the ARK as a double agent spy. Before dawn the scoreboard of war would again show in favor of Adonis and his army.

Chapter 34
Outlier Station

"Fairy tales are more than true. Not because they tell us that dragons exist, but because they tell us that dragons can be beaten."
– Neil Gaiman

Savannah sat in her window nest, surrounded by a pile of blankets and protein bar wrappers. She inhaled deeply, closed her mouth and began to count. *One, one thousand. Two, one thousand. Three, one thousand.* Her record was fifty-three, one thousand. But if the bubble shattered and collapsed, would fifty three seconds be enough to get herself up to the surface?

What if the glass splinters and stabs me when it cracks? She hugged the blanket up closer around her neck. *Twenty-three, one thousand. What if the shadow that comes at night, the one no one else claims to see, wraps itself around me? Will I be strong enough to break free? Will that waste my oxygen and precious seconds? Forty four, one thousand. What did a scream sound like underwater? Did it hurt when icy water filled your lungs? How long before you black out when you are drowning? Fifty… six… one… thousand.*

Savannah gasped for air. Feeling slightly light headed and more than a little satisfied at reaching a new record, she leaned back against the wall and rested her head against the window. As her eyes began to focus and the starbursts of light in her peripheral vision began to fade, she saw the shadow again. Panic gripped her and wouldn't let go.

"It's…" she began in a whisper. "Hurry, come see!" her voice rising quickly. "It's coming!" she screeched backing away from the window pointing. The mothers, used to her panic, moved slowly, but the rest of the crew, not yet desensitized to her dramatics rushed to her side for a look.

"What is that?" Noah asked.

"It's the shadow. I've told you. It comes at night. But no one believes me. It's-"

"It's *Moses*!" Nina shouted. "They're back!"

"No... no, it's..." Savannah said drawing closer to the window.

"You're right!" Noah cheered! "Get the loading dock ready, they are almost here!"

The crew rushed to quickly prepare for their new arrivals while Savannah melted back into her spot, eyes desperately searching the window. *Moses* moved quickly through the water. Unchallenged by even a single predator Mr. Brinestone, with the help of Kurma and his herd, was able to quickly travel the one mile, dock and reunite the members of the crew. They were all welcomed with open arms and cheers of congratulations. Just as the last person departed the submarine, it made an awful screeching noise that finished with an audible pop! Bolts sprung from their places, ricocheting like pinballs inside the small space and sounding like gunshots. Seconds later, streams of water began to shoot into the submarine.

"Well, it did what we needed it to do," Pac said sadly. "But now, it looks like *Moses* is scheduled for a burial at sea. So long friend."

With a sense of sickening Deja vu, the rest of the crew looked on as their chariot of salvation slowly filled with water. Weighted down with its new liquid cargo, the submarine could float no more. Luke and Pac helped Dr. Brinestone disconnect it from the loading dock and together watched it sink to the sea floor, sending up a plume of sea silt as landed.

There would be no escaping tonight and no saving Professor Sorenson either. When the crew registered his missing presence, the look on Flynn's devastated face told them not even to ask.

"Alright, now what?" Noah asked.

"I...," Mrs. Brinestone started and then completed with a phrase rarely heard around the ARK, "I don't know."

"Well, the Outlier Station wasn't meant to support this many people, and especially not for a long period of time. We need to figure out how to get out of here," Mr. Perone reasoned, his brow creased with concern.

"You're right," Mr. Brinestone said perking up. "We're not giving up. Do we have any way to communicate with the Surface Station?"

"Not unless you have something here that works," Flynn began, guiltily remembering her recent battery draining conversation. "We didn't bring anything useful in that department."

"Alright, well let's get started on an escape plan then. We have a dozen or so full oxygen tanks and SCUBA gear here. We will send out two or three groups, in multiple directions and get word to the University that we need rescue assistance," Mr. Brinestone planned. When he saw Luke's hand go up, he shook his head and continued. "Nope, no more children volunteers, the adults go. No questions asked."

"It's not that," Luke began.

"Yeah, we totally agree with your decision to leave us all alone unsupervised... again," Pac said a mischievous smile spread on his face.

"I was just wondering if it wouldn't be helpful to create some sort of diversion to distract the creatures while you make your escape?"

"Excellent thinking," Professor Bebee commented.

"What did you have in mind?"

Luke reached over to his backpack and unzipped it to reveal a case of exploding ink pods from the Obscoral supply closet. "Well we could use these for a start," he said, his face mirroring Pac's.

"Excellent," Mr. Brinestone praised. "We can't guarantee how long this peace period is going to last, so even though it's the middle of the night and we're short on sleep, we better move quickly. Kids, you know these animals better than anyone. Work together to create a distraction plan. The rest of us, let's work over here," he said clearing a spot off at a dining table. Within minutes, plans were formed, routes were plotted, and distractions were arranged. They might be going down, but they weren't going down without a fight.

Chapter 35
ARK

"It's a lack of faith that makes people afraid of meeting challenges, and I believe in myself." – Muhammad Ali

    Slumped against the TUBE wall Professor Sorenson raised his arm again and tapped out a cry for help on the fiberglass tunnel. ---…--- SOS ---…--- SOS. The empty vertical tunnel was an excellent transmitter of sound and his message was carried clear and strong to the surface. When his arm would begin to ache and cramp, he would let it fall and rest in his lap until it relaxed. He repeated the process, alternating arms, through the dark night until first light. The jellyfish guard kept him company, at first only in presence, but when his eyes got heavy and they could see him falling asleep, they began to prompt him with questions, attempting to keep him engaged and awake. The professor happily answered each question, rambling on and on about himself.

    As his cramping arm rested, he talked about the first time he ever envisioned the ARK. Like many successful achievers his dreams started in childhood and continued to grow. Extracurricular activities and clubs supplemented his public school education, preparing him for his four year under graduate degree at Bay City University. A homegrown hero, Bay City was thrilled one of their own, especially a bright and promising student, was a rising star in the academic world.

    Professor Sorenson continued to reminisce aloud during his SOS tapping breaks. The jellyfish mostly listened, but occasionally asked a question and more often reminded him it was time to tap again. It was during one of rambling reminiscences that Simon walked into the Surface Station. Assuming the station would be empty at such early hours, a confused Simon followed the source of the noise to his office and the empty TUBE. Having sat through several of the professor's lectures, Simon instantly recognized his voice and the fact that he was in the middle of a seemingly endless story.

Simon stuck his head into the empty tube and called down. "Umm, Professor? I hate to interrupt, but what exactly are you doing?"

"Ah Simon my boy! Excellent timing!"

"For what?" Simon shouted back down.

"To get me out of here. There's been an attempted coup. It failed, but still, we're in a bit of a pickle. Literally, and if you don't get me out of here, my pickled skin will turn into something far more unpleasant."

"Okay, what do you want me to do?" Simon called.

Professor Sorenson called up instructions in a voice that Simon deemed much too calm for the current situation. Opening the supply closet to the right of the TUBE Simon found the emergency kit. From the giant red duffle bag he pulled a rolled ladder, which he immediately affixed to the TUBE's lower edge. Holding the top hooks with a viselike grip, he pushed the coiled rungs over the edge and watched them cascade down the four hundred foot hole. Once he assured himself that the ladder wasn't going anywhere (specifically down) he returned to the emergency kit to retrieve a long rope. Tying one end to the leg of his desk he then threaded it through a number of other stationary objects before tossing it down the TUBE as well. The professor tied the rope around his portly midsection before shimmying the rope to rest under his armpits. If the climb didn't induce a lethal heart attack, falling four hundred feet to a metal floor would surely kill him.

"Alright Simon. I'm coming up!" With a gigantic grunt the professor heaved himself up onto the first rung of the ladder and began to climb. It was slow going, even with Simon pulling on the safety rope with all of his scrawny strength. For nearly an hour, Professor Sorenson climbed and Simon pulled. Step, heave, reach, pull. Foot after foot, Professor Sorenson escaped from his drowning brainchild, until finally, he was hoisting himself over the edge of the TUBE shaft and collapsing on the Surface Station floor. After both Professor Sorenson and Simon had lain panting for several minutes, the professor rolled over and extended a handshake of thanks.

"Hiring you might have been the best move of my entire career."

"You're welcome," Simon said, a smile spread across his face. "Glad I could help."

Struggling to sit up, the professor grunted unbecomingly and then said, "So here's what we need to do next."

Twenty minutes later, they left the Surface Station, going their separate ways with a plan to meet there again in two short hours. Before then, there was much to do.

Professor Sorenson went straight to his office and with the help of a very startled Mrs. Worthington, contacted the necessary Surface Station staff with instructions to meet at the station at 10 o'clock. He then went home, explained his recent disappearance to his wife, omitting a few details and then took a shower. He felt a little guilty allowing himself this small luxury while his scientists were stranded below. Even though he instructed Mrs. Worthington that not a single news camera was allowed within a one mile radius of the Surface Station, he felt a fresh face, compared to the deranged and haggard face he currently wore, would be a better means of convincing his staff to follow his lead.

For his part Simon did was he did best. He collected supplies for the scientists. A clean set of clothes for each was purchased from the BCU bookstore. A deliciously catered brunch, completely sans-seafood, was set to arrive at the Nelson home promptly at 11am. Fully stocked first aid kits were assembled and an ambulance was on call should it be required.

Operation Rescue was set to commence. The two returned to the Surface Station, their jobs completed earlier than expected and spent their remaining time attempting to contact the Outlier Station. Four hundred feet below, Flynn's converter lay dead on the counter. Even the red charge light was dark, the batteries drained beyond use.

Chapter 36
ARK

"A winning strategy is not about planning. It's about quick responses to changing conditions." – from: The Art of War by Sun Tzu

Unafraid, Marianus swam quickly away, leaving the cave in his wake. Soon the underwater world would be waking and he needed to be to the ARK before then. Along the way he rehearsed what he would tell the allies.

Please, let me in! Adonis has gone crazy! He wants to rule the world! I cannot work for him anymore. I can offer you information, if only you'll let me in. Please, he doesn't know I am here. If one of the dolphin patrols spots me, I'm fish food. Please.

He was confident they would let him in. As he swam his confidence grew, especially now that he was no longer in the dark recesses of the cave with Adonis and the true mastermind behind it all. How scared he had been. Its size alone was enough to make any fish quiver in fear. Marianus pushed his fears from his mind and focused on completing his part of the plan. He counted on the allies being defensive upon his arrival. What he didn't count on was Commander Hale.

"You!" Marianus breathed and backed away from the stout black and gold fish as if his desertion was a disease he could contract.

"I should say that I am also surprised to see you here. Do tell Admiral Marianus," Hale responded coolly, saying his name like a swear word, "what brings you to visit the ARK Allies?"

"I am like you," Marianus began.

"I doubt it," Hale spat, "but continue."

"I have come to trade sides. I have information you

need and I am willing to give it to you for sanctuary."

For a long moment the two stared into each other's eyes, searching for the answers they hoped to find.

"I know I only recently learned to talk, but Jett tells me there is a phrase the humans use often. I think it will serve us well in this situation," Hale said.

"Forgive and forget?" Marianus guessed.

"Better safe than sorry. Guards. Apprehend this creature and lock him a holding chamber. Not one of you should leave until I arrive to set up a prisoner's watch schedule and give further instructions."

"Prisoner?! Commander Hale, you know what he's like! I couldn't take it anymore. He's crazy! Please Hale!" Marianus continued to plead his case as he was dragged further into the ARK and locked into a cell.

Hale momentarily questioned his own judgment. Marianus was right. Adonis was crazy. Shaking his head to clear the confusion, Hale stuck with his gut instinct partnered with the human advice. Until they could get to the bottom of Marianus' appearance at the ARK, he would remain safely locked away. Safe from causing any harm, and also, just in case he was telling the truth, safe from Adonis as well.

Chapter 37
Underwater Cave

"Failure is only the opportunity to begin again more intelligently."
– Henry Ford

"The situation is not under control," Adonis said. "Marianus has gone to the traitors to infiltrate them as a spy, but he was supposed to be back by now." He paced back and forth in the depths of the cave, his anxiety growing. Failure what not an option. Suddenly Adonis felt the swish of a giant tentacle glide past his face and he stopped still to avoid personal injury.

"You should send someone to check on him," said the owner of the tentacle.

"You're right, but who can I trust?" Adonis squeezed his bloodshot eyes tight, unused to the sting of tiredness he felt lurking behind them.

"Let me do this. It's time I took a bigger role. With my camouflage capabilities, I'll be almost invisible."

"Really? You'd do that?" Adonis asked, relief flooding into his voice.

"Of course."

"Oh thank you your highness. I'm doing everything I can… I just… I just…" Adonis failed to finish his sentence.

"It's fine. You've done well. But if I want this revolution to succeed, mistakes can't be made now. Especially without consequence. I'd hate to have to dispense of my figurehead and take charge of the Water Warriors myself." Adonis resisted the urge to whimper and cower in the presence of his leader, but inside, his heart pumped hard and his flight response was firing. Still he stood his ground, his terror internalized.

"I will wait until the cover of night and then check in on our little spy. I'm getting hungry anyway and need to hunt. You will go now on a scouting report of the humans. Maybe pay them a little visit with some friends, if you know what I mean."

"I do and I won't let you down."

"See that you don't. Poseidon knows no wrath like my own."

Adonis swam out from the deep recesses of the cave's catacombs to find his army awake and awaiting orders. Their chatter died instantly as Adonis swam to the front of the group. Mentally tallying his troops Adonis was disappointed to see that they numbered merely half of what they had been the day before. Steadying his nerves after his terrifying encounter, Adonis gazed just above the heads of his commanders, formulating his thoughts. Then he began to tell them the plan.

Assembling a raiding party didn't take long. A few hours after first light Adonis lead the shark guard, the Mahi and the dolphins to the small human dwelling in the middle of the ocean. Without Marianus, it was difficult to command them all at once, but they were only going to harass and take stock of the scene. No larger goal or objective need be completed. Swimming fiercely and boldly through the water their scales and swordfish armor glittered in the morning light.

Chapter 38
Outlier Station

"No one is as capable of gratitude as the one who has emerged from the kingdom of night." – Elie Wiesel

    Professor Sorenson completely skipped the "why" portion when describing the procedures of the rescue operation to his staff of scientists. Judging by the speed and efficiency of the scientists, it was either unnecessary or completely overlooked in their relief to have their beloved leader returned to them in one piece. After a brief plan of action meeting, four fully fueled and loaded mini subs were boarded and quickly submerged in the water. They made a direct path for the Outlier Station. Instructed to kill any creature making an attack, the mini subs were equipped to handle even the deadliest predators. The subs had traveled just yards away from the Surface Station before they were discovered by the Water Warriors.

    The creatures wasted no time making their presence known. Following Adonis' orders Mahi flanked the subs on all sides, their ugly meaty heads obscuring the vision of the scientists inside. If not for the GPS and autopilot within the subs, the mission might have been doomed from the beginning. Unfortunately, this first disturbance was but a hiccup compared to the full on body seizing attack that came next. Just moments before docking at the Outlier Station, the Mahi cleared, only to be replaced by the sharks. Adonis' security guards circled the station and the sub, snapping their jaws full of sharp teeth.

    The ARK crew had not been forewarned of their rescue attempt, but their midnight preparations proved helpful and they jumped into action quickly. For an intense span of several minutes they scuttled about the station waking those who were sleeping and then got into position.

Sonora, Nina, and Noah stood shaking at the loading dock while the first sub boldly swam through the Water Warriors to the Outlier Station. Savannah remained at the window, her head swiveling wildly on her neck, attempting to take in all the action that was happening around and above her. Nina had taken her hand and tried to pull her to the loading dock, but Savannah refused to go. Nina looked back at her now, tears streaming down her face, heartsick for Savannah in her blind panic.

Immediately after the first sub docked, the doors were thrust open and the children were pulled inside forcing Nina to leave Savannah. Right behind them Mrs. Brinestone and several of the other mother scientists rushed inside, arms laden with experiments in progress, specifically the early stages of a PE-328 antidote.

The doors slammed shut and the sub began backing away. Just as they cleared the station a shark rammed its head into the metal sub. Inside muffled screams and panicked pleas to hold steady rang out, their voices magnified as they bounced off the metal walls. The vehicle shuddered against the brute force, but continued to rise slowly to safety. Assured of their own safety as marked by their continued ascent, they rushed to the windows of the sub and watched the action of the battle below.

The second sub circled the station, looking for an opening to enter, but the sharks' menacing jaws and powerfully thrashing tails kept it from docking securely. Suddenly pods of dark ink began exploding in the water. Heads inside the Outlier Station snapped this way and that trying to find the location of the brilliant distraction plan put in action. From a portal window in the sub above, Noah gave a thumbs up as he fed ink pod after ink pod out a fish food dispenser from the bottom of the sub.

Black splotches of octopus ink clouded the water and confused the sharks. Swimming aimlessly without a target, they failed to keep the second sub from docking. The third and fourth subs, armed to the teeth with weapons, took full advantage of the situation and further distracted the predators, allowing the crew to board the sub. Dr. Brinestone stood at the edge of the door and counted his crewmembers as the boys and fathers rushed into the liberating vehicle. It was then he saw Savannah, curled up in her nest, shaking violently with fear and heaving sobs.

"Wait!" he called out. Pac, the second to last to load, followed Dr. Brinestone's horrified line of sight and sprinted across the room. Leaping a couch as if an Olympic hurdler, he was to Savannah in seconds. He ignored her screams and beating fists as he heaved her up and over his shoulders like a sack of seaweed. Laden down by his load he maneuvered around the furniture as he made his way back to the sub. "Good man," Dr. Brinestone said clapping him on the shoulder.

As Pac ducked his head into the sub a violent thud sent him sprawling to his knees and Savannah tumbling from his arms to the floor. When they looked up a bloody shark body slid down the portal window, a harpoon sticking out beneath its fin. Savannah's eyes rolled into the back of her head, flashing a sickly white before she fainted face first on the metal floor. Dr. Brinestone stepped in and over the two sprawled bodies before helping the others to pull Savannah completely within the sub and seal the door. An eerie silence pervaded the cavity of the sub.

With every last scientist and civilian inside the sub, Mr. Brinestone gave the order to surface. From then on, the sharks backed off, but kept a menacing presence nonetheless. The Mahi again flanked the subs for a while, but with the image of the harpooned shark fresh in their minds, they did little else to impede the scientists' journey home. Eventually, deciding their presence was useless, they fell away, leaving the sub to rise and return in peace. As the subs traveled back to the Surface Station, heart rates settled, minds went numbingly blank, tired eyes drooped, and silently the ARK crew was thankful for their rescuers.

When the subs were no longer visible, Adonis let out a heart splitting cry of rage and grief. No commander dared comfort him as he beat himself upon the coral, screaming and shouting incoherently about the failure of yet another plan.

Chapter 39
Surface

"It is not so much our friends' help that helps us, as the confident knowledge that they will help us." – Epicurus

Nora slept past ten for the second day in a row. She wasn't expecting anyone home until dinner time, so when she awoke to the vision of her best friend and sister sitting on the end of her bed, she thought she was dreaming. Nora punched her pillow, rolled over and pulled the covers up over her head.

"I'm gonna need a psych eval before all of this is done," she mumbled into her pillow. "Already the guilt is driving me to hallucinate."

"It's not survivor's guilt if everyone makes it out alive."

"Flynn?" Nora asked without lifting her head from the pillow. "Please tell me you're here and I'm not going crazy."

"Yes, I'm here and so is Nina. But as for crazy, the verdict's still out." Flynn snatched the pillow out from under Nora's mass of tangled hair and smacked her over the head with it. "Now get outta that bed and give us some hugs!"

Nora threw back the covers and rushed out of her bed and into her best friend's arms. When Flynn finally released her, Nina took her turn. For all the differences between the sisters, the time spent apart had erased most of them. Teary eyed the both of them, they hugged away the petty differences they once had.

"What? How? I mean..." Nora started to ask, but couldn't fully form her questions.

"Flynn, will you catch her up to speed? I'm going to go downstairs and see if I can manage the massive brunch Simon just had delivered to feed this house full of people."

"Simon? House full?" Nora asked. Nina nodded and then walked out of the room closing the door behind her. An hour and a half later Flynn and Nora walked downstairs. They weren't totally caught up, but the basic how's had been covered. It was the: "what's", "with who" and the "why's" swimming around in Nora's brain that still remained to be explained.

Chapter 40
Surface

"My words are unerring tools of destruction, and I've come unequipped with the ability to disarm them." – Gansey from The Raven Boys by Maggie Stiefvater

    Mr. and Mrs. Nelson's minivan pulled into the driveway and then entered the garage. They chatted about their lovely weekend getaway as they walked into the house, but their conversation was cut short when their oldest daughter catapulted herself into their arms. As Nora watched her surprised parents take in their full house, a huge smile spread across her face. She relished her chance to hear the details again, the ones she had been so desperately needing these past few weeks. She committed names and faces to memory, as they introduced themselves one by one. She had to suppress a giggle as Caspian nervously greeted Mr. and Mrs. Nelson with a firm handshake while Nina explained that he was her boyfriend.

    Within no time, pizzas covered every inch of counter space and conversations lingered in every corner of the house. For the first time since Flynn left, Nora felt happy and content. If only she ignored the nagging voice in her head that constantly reminded her she had kissed her best friend's ex-boyfriend only hours ago, she could really relax.

*   *   *   *   *

    After every last slice of pizza was eaten and the dishes had long been washed and dried, Nora and Flynn sat on the too- small-for-two-teenage-girls bed. Dressed in their pajamas, they talked about everything and nothing, busy in the moment of being best friends. Alex fully expected to see Nora sitting on her bed alone, so when he burst into her room saying, "I know how we'll tell her, I'll just-" the words died on his lips when he saw Flynn on the bed next to her.

"Tell who what?" Flynn asked, the same time Nora asked "Who let you in?"

"Your mom," Alex answered.

"What do you need to tell your mom?" Flynn turned to ask Nora. Alex, eyes wide, shook his head no, and Nora sighed. Ignoring Alex's silent protestations, she focused fully on Flynn. She took a deep breath and dove into the turbulent conversation.

"I want you to know that yesterday was the absolute most horrible day of my entire life, but it still doesn't excuse what I did."

"Whatever it is, it can't be that bad," Flynn assured her.

"Alex kissed me," Nora confessed and Flynn gasped. "And I kissed him back. I'm so sorry. To both of you." Nora's eyes filled with tears and flicked between the two of them. "Alex has been the only one who's been here for me through this whole thing and I just, I just..." Nora didn't know how to finish the sentence. "And Alex, I am so thankful to you, for everything, but I don't like you like that. Last night was just – just..." again she fell silent. "I so so sorry. God! Why does everything keep getting so screwed up?!" she sobbed. Flynn stood up, and backed away from the bed. Her eyes volleyed between the two silent faces that looked at her pleadingly.

"I'm sorry I was stuck at the bottom of the ocean battling psycho mammals on a power trip instead of shopping up here on the surface with you! I'm sorry your life has super sucked lately! I'm sorry that you don't demand the attention you deserve! But this," Flynn said pointing between Alex and Nora, "This is inexcusable." She walked out of the room, down the stairs, past the gathered crowd in the living room and out the front door.

Chapter 41
ARK

"A lie can travel halfway around the world while the truth is putting on its shoes." – Mark Twain

In two days' time an invitation would be delivered. The Allies were going to be requested to come to Adonis' headquarters to retrieve a supply of the changing solution. The Water Warriors were threatening to spread the changing solution far and wide, unless the ARK Allies agreed to parlay with Adonis and his army. Marianus reported that Adonis planned to make the humans engineer him a new batch, but if that could not be done, the supply from within the ARK would be stolen. Whether the ARK would be attacked or a spy lay hidden in wait to take it, Marianus could not confirm. Either way, once the allies were assembled at the mouth of the cave to rescue the solution and participate in the insinuated treaty discussions, the attack would begin.

Marianus told 'Cuda and Jett all this and more from within his prisoner's cell in the ARK. Jett didn't even need to persuade his captive to speak, his tentacles hung crackling with unused power, while Marianus' words flowed on and on. When Jett was certain that Marianus had told them all he could, they exited the cell.

Confident that the brainless jellyfish and barracuda duo had believed the lies he'd just told, Marianus sunk to the floor. His nervous adrenaline spent, he lay exhausted in his cell. Marianus hoped they brought every last ARK Ally to the rendezvous; that way they could wipe them all out in one smooth swipe. There was no way they could survive what Adonis had in mind. In fact, Marianus wondered nervously, once the attack began, if any of them would survive. Relieved that thus far things were going exactly to plan, Marianus relaxed for the first time in days.

"This thinking like a human business is hard work," he mumbled to himself. Momentarily grateful for the safe haven of his prison, he closed his eyes and drifted into a peaceful sleep.

Just outside the prisoner's cell another barracuda swam up, ready to relieve 'Cuda of his guard duty. While 'Cuda relayed the strict overseeing protocols to the new guard, named Silas, Jett swam off in search of Hale to report their findings. As Jett swam through the flooded halls and passageways the sights were familiar, but exciting from his new eyelevel vantage point. He was still in awe of his new found freedom and prized the journey through the ARK. He knew it saddened the humans, but in his opinion, the ARK had never been better. As he swam past the observation deck he skirted the edges of the room, trying to avoid his parents if possible. He didn't have time to get into another argument right now.

I can't believe they are so shallow minded about this whole thing! he fumed, picking up the debate inside his head. *What's not to love about thinking? And talking! Talking is amazing! But oh no! Not for them!*

Ever since "the change", as Jett's father dramatically called it, his mother Adriel had refused to utter a word. In fact she had refused to even come out of the holding tank where the human boys had played games; even once the ARK was flooded! Jett couldn't understand why his parents were so afraid of change and Jett's father Steve couldn't understand how Jett could love something that made his mother so miserable. So while Jett fought the Water Warriors for his friends and for his own freedom, Steve fought them so that things could return to a natural state as fast as possible.

"Fat chance I'll let that happen," Jett muttered as he rounded a corner and swam straight into Hale.

"Watch it there sparky," Hale said while quickly disentangling himself from Jett's dangerous tentacles.

"Sorry," Jett said, pushing his parental problems out of his mind.

"How's our prisoner?" Hale asked, more than a safe distance away.

"Interesting," Jett began and then filled him in on all the Mahi had said.

Hale was leery of showing up on Adonis' turf. If Adonis really just wanted to talk, then there was no reason why everyone couldn't meet in neutral territory. No, there was definitely something more to his half told story. In addition to his concerns about the meeting location, Hale knew there had been no infiltrations of the ARK. The changing solution still remained safely guarded within the ARK and he told Jett so. Jett was about to swim away when Hale said he had more to say.

"You aren't the only one with news. Our boundary patrol returned with reports that there was a skirmish between the Water Warriors and the humans at the Outlier Station. It was bloody, but ended well. The humans have safely escaped to the surface."

"Are they okay?" Jett asked, concern for his friends clearly expressed.

"According to the patrollers they earned a few bumps and bruises, but they got away without any major harm."

"Good. So what do we do now?" Jett asked his leader.

"Find Pelamis and tell him to prepare to journey to the surface tomorrow, to tell the humans of our current situation with the prisoner Marianus. We will wait a while longer to see how things play out, and get feedback from the surface before diving into any decisions." Jett nodded his bulbous head, mentally noting each of Hale's orders. "Swim safe," he nodded in finality.

"Swim strong." Jett completed the customary motto

before swimming off in search of the snake colony within the ARK while Hale moved in the opposite direction to check the security of the changing solution.

Chapter 42
Surface

"In new situations, all the trickiest rules are the ones nobody bothers to explain to you. (And the ones you can't google.)" – Cath from FanGirl by Rainbow Rowell

Luke caught up with her two blocks later. He was slightly panting as he jogged up behind her and then fell in step.

"Hold up Flynn! Slow down, my sea legs aren't adapted for power walking yet." Flynn slowed bit and together they walked in silence under the clear night sky. After a block or two he said, "I totally get what you were saying about that star thing. This sky view, totally wave rocking."

"If you're gonna live on land, you're going to have to give up the sea slang," Flynn instructed.

"Alright, what should I say?" Luke asked, interested more in keeping Flynn talking than fitting in on land.

"It's epic. The kids up here love that word."

"Epic," Luke tried it out. "Okay, what else?"

As they walked around the Nelson's neighborhood Flynn taught Luke the ways of the surface world. The best restaurant in the mall food court. The way to wear jeans properly, a little baggy, but not overly so, as opposed to the form fitting wetsuits he was used to. The importance of sunscreen and the cool factor of sunglasses. He soaked in her knowledge and attention equally.

"So, do you want to talk about your sudden need for a night time stroll?" Luke asked after Flynn had calmed down.

"Ugh," Flynn sighed and Luke winced. But he didn't pressure her. He just walked, right next to her. "Ugh. Alright,"

Flynn continued. "That guy that just walked into the house?"

"The blonde beach babe?"

"Yes, thank you for reminding me," she said and gave a playful punch to Luke's shoulder. "Anyway, that's my ex-boyfriend."

"I see," Luke commented, carefully keeping his voice even.

"No you don't. I mean not really. Last night Nora kissed him, or he kissed her and she kissed him back and… and… I don't know, but I had to get out of there."

"Dude, rough wake."

"Totally sucks."

"Right, my bad. Totally sucks," Luke corrected himself and was thrilled when he caught a glimmer of a smile on Flynn's lips. "So do you hate them now?"

"No!" Flynn gasped.

"So how long do you want to be mad at them?"

"Him? I don't know. Her?" Flynn let the question hang in the air. "I wish I was done being mad at Nora five minutes ago."

"Then do it. Be done," Luke said, his shoulder shrug suggesting it was no big deal.

"Simple as that?" Flynn asked and stopped walking to turn and face him. In that moment she looked at him like he held all the world's answers. He loved that she looked at him that way.

"If you want it to be," he said grabbing both of her hands in his.

"I do." She squeezed his hands once, gave him a hug and then turned back toward the Nelson's house.

Flynn marched back into the house, leaving Luke in the living room while she took care of her personal business. When she couldn't find Nora in the kitchen, bedroom or backyard she knew exactly where to go. She jogged the few blocks to the public beach. The chill in the air surprised her.

She had never lived through a Florida winter above water and the cool temperature only reminded her that an entire world still waited to be rediscovered.

She found Nora sitting on the beach, staring at the waves. Flynn took a seat directly in front of her best friend, obscuring her ocean view.

"I should be totally pissed at your right now," Flynn said and Nora nodded. "For a long time." Nora nodded again. "You should never have kissed him."

"I know. I'm sorry." Tears slipped from Nora's eyes and tracked down her cheeks.

"I know you are. And I also know that being mad at you is way worse than anything else."

"Really?" Nora's voice squeaked.

"Really," Flynn said and pulled Nora in for a big hug. In a mess of tears and snot and sand all was forgiven.

For the second time that day Nora was living a waking dream, hugging her best friend, in a world that looked so much better than it had the night before. Now, if only they could solve the problem of the pesky animal hostile takeover. But as far as Nora was concerned, that problem could wait until morning.

Chapter 43
Underwater

"When we can no longer change a situation, we are challenged to change ourselves." – Viktor Frankl

For Hale living among the ARK Allies was not all that different from the life he had been living on the coral reef. A multitude of creatures had always shared his living space. Some were friendly and some wanted to eat him, so not even the current war seemed all that unfamiliar to him. Everything was pretty much the same except that it was loud. So loud. So many voices. So many opinions. And somehow it had become his job to listen to them all and decide what to do. What to do. What to do? When the time came, would he know what to do?

For Jett, living among the other sea creatures was a fairy tale come true. His entire life before "the change" had been confined to cramped quarters with only his parents for company. Now, he had not only the humans as friends, but hundreds of jellyfish and countless other creatures. For Jett the change was the best thing that had ever happened to him. The fact that it was his job to deliver messages swimming far and wide and even (gasp!) outside the ARK was perhaps the best part of all. Every day was filled with new faces and new friends. Every new day was the best day of his life and he couldn't wait to see what tomorrow would bring.

For Pelamis living among the ARK Allies was a choice of necessity. The decision to move his herd from their home in the kelp forest to the humans' glass bubble was an agonizing one. And what if he chose wrong? What if he let down those who depended on him to lead them and keep them safe? What if they could have ignored the battle that raged beyond their forest and live peacefully independent and unattached?

What if this whole thing went out with the tide and was gone tomorrow? But in the end, it was the only choice. The danger was too unpredictable and at least inside the bubble the Allies could share the burden of war. His job as message courier between the allies and the humans was a dangerous one, but one he did for his herd. He ignored the fact that he was at the same time helping the humans because if he focused on that he would quit right then and there. No matter how you looked at it, the humans were the ones who had gotten them into this mess. Not Pelamis. But he would get them out of it. He would make it safe again.

For 'Cuda living in the post-human ARK was slightly depressing. He missed Capsian. And little Noah. He knew there were some creatures among the group of allies that strongly disliked the humans – their presence, their influence, their noise. But 'Cuda was not a member of that camp. He often wondered what Caspian was doing up on the surface. Was Flynn missing the ocean even a little bit? What shenanigans were Pac and Luke up to? Was Nina happy to be back home? Maybe next time Pelamis made a journey to the surface he'd volunteer to tag along as security duty. Maybe then he could see Caspian.

For Marianus living among the enemy was just another badge of honor showcasing his loyalty to Adonis. Never had someone needed him so much, trusted him so much. He would do whatever Adonis needed. He strived to never let him down. He had risen from a lowly bottom feeder to a star in the center ring of the circus. He was Admiral Marianus, second in command! All the commanders and warriors knew his name and he loved it. Adonis called him first and him last and sometimes in between. The imprisonment and lies and the worrying. The double crossing and the plotting and the worrying. They were worth it. He swore to himself Adonis was worth it.

For Adonis, living among the Water Warriors was

lonely. With the dolphin pod of his youth he felt like he belonged, like together life was a wonderful game… swimming in the crystal waves, splashing in the warm sunshine, and taking care of each other. But now it was different. He was different. And he couldn't go back to the way things were no matter how badly he wanted to. The sleepless nights. The pressure. The planning. The stakes. The ever-looming threat of failure. They were all too much. Sometimes he thought about going back. But the unpredictable consequences kept him from changing his course. He was different and was sure he could never go back to the way things were before.

Chapter 44
Surface

"This is the danger in loving. No matter how powerful you are, no matter how many kingdoms you rule, you cannot stop those you love from dying." – from The Tale of Despereaux *by Kate DiCamillo*

The next morning Mr. and Mrs. Grier went to the city morgue. Both Professor Bebee and Professor Sorenson went with them for moral support. Everyone had assumed the worst about Carl, but after Nora had told them about the mysterious news reports surrounding a body found on the beach, Carl's fate was all but confirmed.

Two hours after their departure from the Nelson home, the professors returned alone. The Grier's, appropriately claiming post-traumatic stress and grief, immediately left the morgue for their parents' homes in Philadelphia. Carl's body would be sent to them, where a small memorial service would be held with immediate family only.

No one could fault their decision. In the end it was probably the best choice for everyone. The crew could not however move on, no matter the urgency of their scientific responsibilities, without grieving for the loss of their small community. Later that afternoon, they met, dressed in black, at the pier. Facing the winter sun they offered their condolences, memories and tears to Carl and the sea.

Today they would grieve, tomorrow they would work.

"Carl was my best friend," Anton began. "He knew more about motors than anyone on this planet. I spent almost every waking moment of the last eleven years with him and I will always remember him. Swim safe, swim strong."

Others followed.

"Whenever I see a hot rod magazine or an outboard

motor, I will think of Carl and smile," Luke commemorated.

"Carl was a pioneer in his field. In all of my years of teaching and science I have never seen a mechanical mind like his. The world lost many inventions, innovations and wonders when they lost Carl Grier." Professor Bebee blew a kiss to both the sea and sky and the resumed her place among the mourners.

"Carl was a team player and a good friend," Caspian spoke in an emotion filled voice. He had waited until the end, not sure how to put into words the guilt he felt at not being able to have changed the outcome of their mission. "I admire his honesty, his hard work and his passion for his field of science. He will be missed. And I'm sorry. I'm sorry." Nina stood next to him, holding his hand, her brown bangs and tears blurring her vision.

The makeshift funeral procession walked down the boardwalk in silence. A disturbance in the water drew them back to the end of the pier. On bended knee Caspian leaned down to look into the water, the others gathering behind him.

"We heard your voicesss," Pelamis began, his tounge flicking quickly in and out, attempting to assess if any danger lay nearby. "We are sssorry for your losss."

"Thank you Pelamis. How are things below?" Caspian asked.

"At a bit of a ssstand ssstill," the snake said. He continued to tell the crew the details of the situation. The ARK still remained firmly in the Allies' control, and for now, it seemed the Water Warriors had returned to their hideout and were remaining out of sight, with one exception. Pelamis relayed Hale's message – a mixture of facts and opinions, orders and questions.

Caspian thanked him for the information and a plan was made to meet again soon. When the snake disappeared back into the water the funeral party recessed to the waiting cars, their hearts heavy and their minds full of questions.

Chapter 45
Surface

"Here in a small town where it feels like home, I've got everything I need, and nothing that I don't." – from: Homegrown by Zac Brown Band

"Not that I'm complaining about being back on the surface," Flynn started, twirling a bit of fettuccini around her fork, "but now that we are up here, we have no idea what is going on down there. Pelamis clearly pointed that out this afternoon."

"You're right. We've been on the surface two full days and it's like we put the war on pause, but we can be sure Adonis is not doing the same," Luke agreed. Faces around the kitchen nodded in agreement, mouths too full to respond verbally. Every available chair was filled, from the island to the dining room table. Still some ate standing, clustered around counter tops, choosing to be a part of the group rather than eat separately in another room.

"I might be able to help with that," Simon said from across the kitchen.

"Hey, delivery boy!" Flynn said surprised. "What are you doing here?"

"Nora invited me," Simon said sheepishly.

"Oh," Flynn said, curiosity in her voice and her eyes that she leveled at a blushing Nora. "Well what did you have in mind?"

"I have been working on an undercover water camera," Simon explained.

"Sorry to burst your bubble dude, but that's nothing new," Pac said.

"Yeah, I know, but this one is. I mean, it's a camera

inside of an animated fish. It can like, move on its own via remote control and film whatever is around it," Simon finished.

"Now that is new," Professor Sorenson spoke up, dishing himself a second helping and Simon glowed in his praise.

"I have a prototype at my dorm room. I could bring it by the Surface Station tomorrow after class," Simon offered.

"I'm an old man Mr. Ludkin. If I've learned anything from these past few weeks it's that waiting is a fool's game. After dinner we'll go get it and have a look at it tonight."

Simon nodded and then went back to his dinner. Flynn continued to watch Nora, as if discovering an entirely new side to her best friend. Dinner was finished, dishes were done, and the mass of people moved from the kitchen to the living room.

Mr. and Mrs. Nelson continued to take the entire crazy scenario in stride. While the entire Brinestone family remained living in the Nelson home, the rest of the scientists and their families were staying at Professor Sorenson's mansion on the University Campus. Most meals were served there as well, catered by university staff, paid for by university money, but for whatever reason, dinner always seemed to end up at the Nelson home. Perhaps it had more of a homey feel than the pristine and museum like atmosphere of the Sorenson mansion. Perhaps the Brinestone family was the magnet that pulled them all together. Perhaps they were all so entrenched in their scheduled way of life that they continued to follow the same pattern day after day after day.

Several hours after dinner, Mrs. Nelson exclaimed that unlike the rest of them, she had an alarm clock to answer to and a 25 minute commute to follow. Claiming her line up of lab reports for tomorrow were more important than late night comedy she kissed the tops of her daughters' heads and made her way upstairs. The party began to disperse, leaving in twos and threes and fours out the Nelson front door. Professor Bebee kissed Mrs. Nelson on the cheek as she walked out the door and thanked her for another lovely evening. Nora and Flynn walked up stairs together, leaving Caspian and Nina deep in conversation on the couch. Noah, never far from his big brother these days, had already fallen asleep next to them, the TV flickering beyond the trio.

"Cover him up when you go?" Mrs. Brinestone asked her eldest son. Caspian nodded and then she reminded him, "Not too late."

Eventually each member of the household, new and established, found their way to bed. Only Simon and Professor remained awake, huddled around the kitchen island, dissecting, improving and reassembling the fish spy-cam that Simon had created. When finally they were satisfied, they shut off the kitchen lights and let themselves out of the house. Feeling confident on the drive back to his dorm, Simon shared a few of this other ideas with the professor, the professor nodding enthusiastically at each in turn. As Simon stood on the curb in front of his dorm and watched the professor drive away, he marveled at the dramatic change in his life. Smiling, he walked back to his room, and as seemed almost habit, fell asleep as soon as his head hit the pillow.

Chapter 46
ARK

"The things that matter most must never be at the mercy of things that mean the least." – Johann Wolfgang von Goethe

First light found Hale opening his eyes in a crowded room. A plethora of fish surrounded him. A multitude of colors and sizes, shapes and forms, all sleeping peacefully under the careful watch of the night guards.

He yawned and stretched his fins, still awed at the new sensations he experienced each day. Exhaustion and guilt, anxiety and joy, comradery and anger – a platter full of new feelings to sample and decode, to accept or reject, to use in conscious decision making. And today, decisions must be made.

Careful not to disturb the sleeping soldiers around him, he exited the sleeping quarters and went to check in with the head of the night guard and security on any new developments during their shift. Then he planned for a quick breakfast with the troops, a visit to their prisoner and a joint representative meeting with Jett, Pelamis, 'Cuda and Kurma. It was going to be a busy, busy day, but Hale hoped it would be a good one.

The reports from the night guard were unremarkable, which Hale took as a positive sign. No news meant nothing new to deal with. Breakfast was quick and practical, eaten in a makeshift mess hall they had set up in the ARK kitchen. The allied soldiers were both confident and cheerful, a combination Hale hoped would continue. Their prisoner remained the same, overly helpful and unpleasantly lacking in credibility. By the time Hale returned to the observation deck to meet the other members of the joint council, they were already waiting for him. Hale silently greeted them with a nod of his head and flicked a fin, motioning for them to follow him to a more private place.

Jett cringed when he saw Hale swim toward the Obscoral Tank and almost swore aloud when he directed them to swim inside. Jett's parents hovered in the far corner, Adriel ingesting her portion of breakfast Steve had brought from the mess hall.

"Please leave us," Hale said in their direction and then turned to face Pelamis, 'Cuda, Kurma and Jett. "Now I have asked you to meet me here because-" Sensing a lack of motion behind him, Hale paused his prepared meeting agenda to again turn and look at Steve and Adriel. "I said you need to leave. You can return after our meeting, but this meeting is closed to top advisors only." Steve looked at Hale with a sad defiance, while Adriel made no movement at all. Appearing neither apologetic nor compliant, she remained in the corner of the tank. "Listen, both of you, I-"

"Hale," Jett interrupted. Annoyance, another new emotion for Hale, flooded his mind and soured his expression. "I'm sorry," Jett continued. "those are my parents."

"Alright, but that doesn't give them special privileges. I asked them to leave."

"I know, it's just," and here Jett locked eyes with his father's, "My mother, she's just so scared. She hasn't left this room since the change. Please don't make her go. She won't talk, doesn't talk! She's terrified. Please Hale, please don't make her go."

Hale turned to look at the now almost colorless and trembling form that was Jett's mother. Pity overpowered the annoyance and then was replaced by compassion.

"It is a big and scary world out there isn't it Adriel?" Hale said. "Of course you may stay." Steve inclined his head toward Hale in thanks and then made to leave. As he swam to the exit he passed closely to Jett and paused.

"Thank you," he said, his voice thick with emotion.

"She's my mom," Jett responded as if it were explanation enough.

His father nodded and then said, "Let me know when you're done and I'll come back and be with her."

"I will."

Steve left the room and for a moment the room was silent. Jett used his body language to clearly communicate with Hale both his gratitude and readiness to move on.

"Alright, like I was saying. I've asked you to be here, to form a council of representatives. We are still a democracy, but you will be a voice for your kind, bringing their needs, opinions, and complaints to the group for consideration. Do you accept this important role?" When they each nodded, Hale continued. "First we must decide what to do with the changing solution. Despite rumors of infiltration and theft, it is currently safe within the bubble."

"But maybe it shouldn't be. Maybe we should get it out of here," Jett suggested.

"I agree we can't be sure it will be safe here, but where will we move it to and how?" Hale asked.

Jett told the council about the TUBE and the way the humans used it to transport themselves and their goods to the surface. Pelamis told of his TUBE experience, adding his vote of confidence toward the plan. Even though it was currently out of commission, Hale quickly saw it as the best possible solution within their grasp.

"We will contact the humans and work to get this TUBE back in working order as fast as possible," Hale confirmed. "Pelamis, are you willing to deliver another message?"

The snake nodded in agreement. "They are expecting to hear from us again at last light."

"Excellent. Make preparations for your travel. Meeting adjourned."

Hale left the room first, his mental to-do list already

onto the next task. Pelamis followed him out the door, eager to relay the news to his herd. 'Cuda left to make sure the night guards were replaced with fresh barracuda bodies, fully fueled from a night's sleep and breakfast. Kurma gave Jett a reassuring smile and then gestured for him to go talk to his mother. Jett did his best impression of Pac's teenage sheepish shrug and then followed the wise turtle's advice. Kurma patted him on the head, received a sharp shock, winced and then left.

At first Jett didn't know what to say. He hung next to her, sharing only space and nothing more. Slowly he reached out a tentacle toward her and then entwined it with hers.

"I'm sorry this is so hard for you," he began. "I'm sorry if I've made it harder. We are working, I am working, to end it. I hope you can forgive my friends for doing this to you. I hope you can forgive me." Adriel looked up at her son and spoke her first words.

"I do."

"Thank you!" Jett said, the relief in his voice strong. "Just do me a favor? Don't let anyone else know you talk, or I might have to let you get kicked outta here next time." Adriel nodded and leaned in, giving her son a warm embrace. He squeezed her tentacle once more and then turned to leave. He met his father on his way out of the tank. Knowing that nothing more needed to be said, they passed each other wordlessly, at peace with each other for the first time in weeks.

Chapter 47
Surface

"You can't build a reputation on what you are going to do."
– Henry Ford

When he first poked his scaly head out of the water at the pier, he was greeted by four others. Actually, Luke, Pac, Flynn and Nora were thoroughly engrossed in star gazing, pointing out a variety of constellations just beginning to become visible in the evening sky, so Pelamis had to hiss for several minutes before they took notice of him. When they finally did see him and pay attention it was only to tell him to travel across the bay to the Surface Station where he could meet with Caspian and the others in sheltered safety.

Pelamis cursed the frolicking foursome as they lay down on the dock, their arms stretching skyward, continuing their astronomy discussion. He slid back underwater and traveled the treacherous miles to the new meeting location. To be fair, the welcome party had offered to transport him by land, but Pelamis strongly refused. Only pets belonged in tanks, and even then, he wasn't so sure. One time in a plastic bag was one time too many in his opinion. So across the bay he swam, sticking to the shadowy shore as much as possible. At last he arrived and could communicate the allies' message.

The second time his head broke the water's surface Pelamis looked up into the faces of Caspian, Dr. Brinestone and Professor Sorenson. The glass and steel of the Surface Station surrounding them was not all that different from the underwater version four hundred feet below.

"We are nervousss the Water Warriorsss are planning an attack, or worssse that there is a traitor in our midsssst planning to ssssteal the transsssforming sssolution." The humans listened intently. "We think moving it to the sssurface is the bessst way to keep it sssafe."

"Do you have a plan on how you'd like to proceed?" Dr. Brinestone asked.

"Yesss. If posssible we would like to sssend it up. Jett hasss told usss thisss could be done with the help of sssomething you call the TUBE."

"It would take us a few hours to get it back in working order, but it can be done," Professor Sorenson assured.

"Excellent. Do it."

The details of when and how were further discussed. A short time later Pelamis was ready to depart. Caspian tried to convince Pelamis to travel back down through the TUBE once fully reflooded, but he refused, bartering his own safety for the prompt relay of useful information to the ARK Allies. Guiltily, Caspian watched him swim away, his mental turmoil ebbing only slightly when he saw two turtles nearby awaiting to guide and guard him on his way back down.

Pelamis sped through the dark waters, the turtles flanking him on either side. Just once a dark shadow passed quickly below them, causing them to flinch. It moved on quickly, clearly having something other than an attack or quick meal on its mind. Pelamis breathed a sigh of relief when they reached the kelp forest and obscurely drifted down through their concealing vines. He missed his home dearly and treasured the not so small comfort of visiting. He knew many others were not so lucky.

After their descent through the kelp came the most dangerous part of the journey: the one mile swim through the open ocean back to the ARK. On their way to the surface, they had twice needed to stop and hide next to rocks or drop into the sand, burying themselves to keep from being seen. Now it was dark and it would be easier for them to hide. But the same could be said of their enemies.

Staying low, Pelamis took the lead and edged out of the

gently swaying kelp fronds. Quickly the threesome traveled, skimming the sand, their destination inching closer minute by minute. By the time they saw the bioluminescent glow of the ARK reach its fingers of light out across the sea floor, Pelamis was almost convinced they'd made their return without any major event. He swished his tail ready to propel himself the final meters to safety when a sudden noise stopped him. He hung suspended in the water, his tongue flicking feverishly trying to sense any danger.

Chapter 48
Surface

"I hope you spend your days and they all add up."- from: I Lived by One Republic

    The high school gym crackled with excitement that Flynn was sure would register on an electrometer. The parents, certain that science was stealing their children's childhood, forced them out of the Nelson family front doors with strict instructions not to return before ten PM. The adults asserted that they were fully capable of returning the TUBE to working order, and that nothing else could be accomplished until the morning. When Caspian tried to argue the adults firmly held their ground, insisting this was a mandatory "night off". Nina pulled him down the driveway and then to the sidewalk, where they followed in the wake of happy chatter from the rest of the group.

    Upon entering the gym, Flynn was a star reborn. Friend and foe alike flocked to her side, demanding her attention, story and part of her interstellar shine. A few months ago she'd have been pulled into their orbit, but tonight she grabbed Nora and Luke's hands and led them to a clear spot on the bleachers the rest following behind. It wasn't long before Pac and Luke stole her limelight. Rivaling even the rowdiest Bay City fans, they stood clapping, stomping and cheering. They spurred on the Baracudas with the same enthusiasm they poured into the rest of their lives. The only difference now was that they had a visible and vocal outlet.

    The horn sounding half time blared and the student section took their seats. Attention turned from the game to each other. Flynn leaned over to Luke and said, "I think you've missed your calling as a male cheerleader."

"They have those?" he responded excitedly before tossing her a playful wink and a delicious smile. Flynn blushed and nudged him with her shoulder. Her response was interrupted when Pac crawled his way over both Anton and Nora to squish himself between Luke and Flynn.

"Looks like somebody is a little jealous his bromance is being disrupted," Nora teased Flynn.

"Shut up!" Flynn hissed so only Nora could hear.

"Dude, dude!" Pac said in a stage whisper. "That girl is totally checking me out!"

"Which one?" Nora asked excitedly.

"That one," Pac said pointing across the gym. Nora's smiled faded completely.

"Dude," Nora said mockingly. "That girl, is Savannah."

"What?!? No way!" Pac exclaimed. "The crazy shadow girl from the Outlier Station? She looks so different!"

"You mean she looks so dangerous," Flynn corrected. "Pac, trust me. You don't want that, no matter how bright the sequins shine."

"Talk about a habitat changing a creature!" Pac turned to look at Nora and Nina in awe. "You surface girls are something else." He crawled his way back to his original spot and a short time later half time was over.

At first Nora thought Savannah was just keeping a close eye on her social enemies, but Pac was right. Each time Nora looked, Savannah was staring straight at Pac. Her eyes were glittering gems, cold and hard, with only one target. Something was up, and when Savannah was involved, it wasn't usually something good. A bad feeling began growing in Nora's gut. She tried to convince herself it was too much popcorn and Skittles, but she had a hard time believing her own logic.

After a nail biting fourth quarter, the Barracuda's pulled off and exciting 58-55 victory. Riding the wave of enthusiasm all the way to the PitStop, the crew soon found themselves surrounded by chocolate malts, French fries and dramatic live replays of the game, compliments of the team's two new biggest fans.

Luke had just gotten done lifting Noah as he mimed a dunk (which hadn't actually happened in the game) when the tarnished bell above the front door jingled to life. Nora snapped her head up looking for Simon out of habit. She was disappointed when he didn't walk through the door. She was highly annoyed when Savannah and Kelsey did.

"I said wait outside Kelsey!" Savannah snapped. "God, it's like that girl can't breathe her own air," she mumbled as she took a seat at the fringe of the group.

"You never seemed to mind before," Nora said not nicely, watching Kelsey slink back out the door and do as she was told.

"Yeah, well things are different now," Savannah snapped again, although this time with a little less bite. A haunted look could still be seen in her heavily make up covered eyes. Behind the mascara and glitter, she was still more than a little scarred.

"I suppose you're right," Nina responded eyeing her sister.

"What brings you to the Pit Stop?" Nora asked, ignoring her sister's pleading look to play nice.

"I came to talk to him," Savannah said pointing at Pac. When he raised his eyebrows in surprise she continued. "I just wanted to say thank you." She paused and then in a rush finished, "For not leaving me behind."

"Totally welcome babe," Pac responded. He raised his hand, for a customary high five and Savannah rolled her eyes, her store of gratitude apparently depleted.

"Right, well, enjoy the milkshakes," she said and left them all momentarily speechless. Pac shrugged before saying, "See? I told you. Surface girls are all kinds of weird."

"Caspian, you can stop searching for that eighth

wonder of the world for your thesis," Flynn said sarcastically. "Because that was just it." The group erupted in laughter, causing Savannah to toss a nasty glance over her shoulder. And just like that the social hierarchy of the high school world was righted again.

Chapter 49
ARK

"Everybody is a genius. But if you judge a fish by its ability to climb a tree, it will live its whole life believing it is stupid." – Albert Einstein

"Pst."

He heard the noise again. This time the turtles heard it too and began looking around for the source of the noise. *We are so close!* Pelamis thought, *Will we really be thwarted now that we have made it all this way?* The sound of his own frightened heartbeat echoed in his tiny ears. If it weren't for the subtle shift of the sand, he might not have noticed where the next words came from.

"Pst. Down here." A flash of pink and orange peeked out from beneath the sand and Pelamis relaxed considerably when he saw it was merely a starfish.

"Thisss place isss not sssafe," Pelamis whispered. "If you wisssh to ssspeak with me, prove your loyalty by ssswimming to the bubble."

A beat of uncertainty passed and then Pelamis darted forward. The turtles followed his lead and caught up quickly. The little starfish followed behind, as fast as nature would allow her to swim. Arriving several yards ahead of the starfish, Pelamis quickly assembeled a security detail to surround the bright star as it entered their complex. Standing trial to their jury, the small star began to speak.

"My name is Aster," she began. "I represent the local constellation of sea stars and starfish." Pelamis nodded and she continued. "We would like to join the Allies in their fight."

Pelamis peered at the tiny creature, wondering how she and her kind could possibly aid their mission. A larger part of him wondered if this was the trap they had been warned of and were waiting to surface. He hoped to fish out the answer with a single question.

"Why have you waited ssso long to choossse a ssside and come forward?"

"With all due respect, we have been around for 450 million years. We hardly thought we were going anywhere. Rather than make a hasty decision, or a decision at all, we waited and watched."

"And what have you ssseen?" Pelamis asked, his curiosity uncharacteristically getting the better of him.

"We have seen the great grey dolphin and the trouble he causes. We have heard the clashing of swords. We have smelled the fear in his own army and we have tasted blood in the water."

Those allies surrounding the starfish soaked in her revelations, hanging on every word. Those passing by stopped to hear her speak. As the crowd grew, more were drawn in. Before long it seemed as if all the allies were gathered and present.

"You have contributed to none of the chaos that brews in these waters. Not even the humans can say that. Our bodies contain many overlapping parts, making us incredibly strong and useful in many capacities. We are fearless. Wear us as armor or use us to reinforce your deteriorating bubble. If we lose an arm, we regenerate a new one. We will be forever useful."

The allies turned as one body to look at Pelamis. Fortunately for the snake, Hale had arrived.

"There have been reports of an enemy attack, an attempt to steal the changing solution and further spread the chaos as you call it," Hale voiced clearly from the back of the crowd. He moved forward and the crowed parted to let him pass until he stood in the center of assembly with Aster and Pelamis. "Who is to say that you are not the enemy of whom we have been warned?"

"We are strong, but our strength lies in our defensive skills and nothing more. Even if we wanted to, we could not harm you."

"And if we don't accept you into our alliance?" Hale further questioned.

"We will return to the unheard of hidden locations from which we have come and wait for this calamity to pass like the many that have come before."

Hale looked to Pelamis who's appraising gaze had not left the starfish since her arrival. He gave a firm nod of approval.

"Allies!" Hale called out. "Before you is Aster, representative of her kind. They wish to aid our side, dedicating their bodies to our cause. Pelamis and I find her loyal and true, brave and strong. But this army is not made of two minds. It is made of many! What say you about their acceptance into our beloved brotherhood?"

Marianus both heard and felt the reverberations of the allies' welcoming cheer. His earlier contentment evaporated, leaving feelings of confusion in their place. *What had just happened? Was this part of Adonis' plan? Did this change his course of action? What would he say when they questioned him?* He'd told them he had all the answers, all the information, but with Adonis that was never quite true.

Instinctively he looked around for direction from Adonis. Solitude met him in every corner of his cell. He was alone. Alone and answerless. *But I can't fail Adonis. Of that much I am certain. Maybe it is time to take things into my own fins. Take charge. Show Adonis I can handle the situation. Yes, yes. That's what I will do. At first light. I have the entire night to plan, but at first light I will act, and Adonis will be proud.*

**Chapter 50
Surface**

"I suppose I could have struggled through without you. But thank heavens I didn't have to." – Pam Brown

Since the Brinestone family had joined her own, Mrs. Nelson's grocery list more than doubled. Flynn's favorite cereal and the Brinestone's preferred blend of coffee. Chicken nuggets for Noah, who after tasting them for the first time swore he'd never eat anything else again. Personally Mrs. Nelson was floored he had gotten through ten years of childhood without a chicken nugget. When Mrs. Brinestone expressed her concern over Noah's new food obsession Mrs. Nelson assured her he would be fine. As both a mom and a professional outside of the home, she was certain her own girls had probably survived for weeks at a time on little more. Somehow though, she didn't feel the message was well received because from that point on, Mrs. Brinestone accompanied her to the grocery store, frequently tossing in sushi, tofu and a variety of other lean meats.

Whether it was their dual grocery shopping or their long post-dinner chats, the two women grew quite close despite having absolutely nothing in common other than being mothers. They became fast friends as they managed the controlled chaos that reigned inside the Nelson household. Mrs. Brinestone used her scientific prowess to set up a strict bathing, laundering and sleeping schedules, not to mention chore rotations, to minimize their inconvenience on their hosts.

Used to an overly organized way of life, the Brinestone family complied without complaint. Shower at 8:30 pm? No problem. Do laundry at four in the afternoon? Got it covered.

Garbage out on Tuesday mornings? Yep. Vacuum before Mrs. Nelson got home from work on Fridays? Done.

When Nora came down for breakfast she was a little surprised to see a full kitchen. Flynn told her they had big plans at the Surface Station today and needed an early start, thus the cramped conditions of the kitchen.

They, Nora thought. *Meaning the Brinestones and Nina. They, like not including me.* Nora turned to plead her case one last time, but before her mouth could fully form the words her mother said,

"I don't want to hear it Nora. You are going to school and that's that." Nora slumped into a recently vacated stool at the island and realized it was very difficult to both pout and eat a bowl of cereal at the same time.

Like every topic of conversation in the past month and a half, it was hotly debated whether the children would go to public school while they spent time on the surface. The logistics involved in handling the underwater situation all made the practicality of attending class impossible. Even Nina was spared the daily dose of education, under the argument that her time in the exchange program was cut short and there was still so much for her to learn through the repair process. The only person who would be attending school besides Nora was Noah.

Nora was highly annoyed. Noah was pumped. Flynn didn't know how to feel. She knew Nora was beyond bummed. While she wanted to make her friend happy, and it would have been fun to go back to the social scene she had desperately fought to join, another part of her was happy to avoid the drama and have the time to focus on fixing the experimental damage that continued to wreak havoc below the water's surface.

Each morning after Nora and Noah left for school, and Mrs. Nelson left for her job at the hospital's genetics lab, the rest of the household made their way over the to the Surface

Station to begin their work again.

    Dr. and Mrs. Brinestone, along with their eldest son and Professor Bebee, headed a team of individuals working on an antidote to the PE-328. Stillman, Sonora and their parents lead lectures for another group of surface scientists on the dramatic changes in the aquatic animals exposed to the infamous solution. Flynn used her technical know-how to help Professor Sorenson and Simon connect the fish-cam, to the Surface Station's digital monitoring system. Luke, Pac and Nina were sent to sit outside the TUBE while it slowly refilled, monitoring its progress and watching for early signals of incoming deliveries.

    Before the sun had fully risen in the sky, the good guys on land were back in working order, ready to battle in this war of science and nature.

Chapter 51
ARK

"Loose lips sink ships all the damn time." – Taylor Swift

"Sir I have news to report," a barracuda said as he approached Hale at breakfast. Despite his initial inward grimace Hale smiled and invited the night guard named Silas to eat with him. Throughout the meal the guard told of Marianus' strange nocturnal behaviors: excessive pacing and mumbling, followed by a restless sleep.

"What was he saying?" Hale asked.

"Well when he was awake, he was careful to keep most of it to himself. But I'm guessing good ol' Adonis didn't count on sending us a sleep-talker as his spy." Twin grins split the fishes' faces in half.

"Tell me everything," Hale said experiencing a rush of excitement and gratitude.

"He's going to try to escape," Silas explained. He continued to relay Marianus' plans to Hale. When he had told all that he knew he said, "So? What do you want us to do? He'll be attempting to leave any minute now."

Hale pondered the state of affairs for a moment in silence, ignoring the increasing and apparent anxiety growing in the guard. He swallowed a bit of breakfast, cleared his throat and then in a hushed tone told Silas exactly how to handle the situation. Silas' eyes bulged as Hale continued to speak.

"But Sir. I don't understand, why?"

"Do you trust me Silas?" Hale asked seriously.

"Absolutely."

"And do you understand the steps I am asking you to take?" Hale pressed.

"Yes, but,"

"Good, that's all you need then. I will explain everything later. The rest of the allies will be gathered on the west side of the bubble. There will be no one to interrupt or interfere with our plan."

"Yes sir, Hale sir," Silas said stoically.

"Good. Swim safe,"

"Swim strong."

The guard left the way he came, leaving with a full belly and a head full of instructions, not to mention more than a few questions. Hale finished his breakfast, feeling satisfied. His plan, in its infancy, was beginning to more fully form in his newly complex brain. On his way out of the mess hall he touched base with his council of representatives and told Jett, Pelamis, 'Cuda and Kurma to gather everyone at the TUBE in a half hour. Aster, the newest of their organization, he would need to arrive as soon as possible.

Chapter 52
Underwater Cave

"The question isn't who is going to let me, it's who is going to stop me." – Ayn Rand

She had not lied to Adonis. At least not this time. She would go to the ARK to check on Marianus, but first she had other business to attend to. It felt good to get out of the cave, swimming and stretching in the wide open ocean. Gliding through the water she let her thoughts stray from the troubles that populated her brain. Instead she focused her attention on her surroundings, her excitement growing the closer she got to the continental shelf and the drop she knew was coming.

Finally she crested the ridge and dove down deep into the dark water. Her attention again shifted, looking now for a creature instead of a location. It was not a meal she searched for. She had feasted on her way, snatching her meal as she swam through the water. It was something else she hungered for.

Back and forth she swam. Up and down the canyon. Searching. Time was running out. It had to be tonight. Everything would be for nothing if she failed in this task. At last she found him. Wordlessly she took from him what she needed, and swam away satisfied.

Chapter 53
ARK

"Listen to the musn'ts child, listen to the don'ts. Listen to the shouldn'ts, the impossibles, the won'ts. Listen to the never haves then listen close to me… Anything can happen child, anything can be." – Shel Silverstein

Silas found Marianus exactly how he had left him, pacing in the cell. As he entered the cell the flash of his silver scales startled Marianus. The already jumpy fish darted to the back of his holding tank.

"Just bringing you some breakfast," Silas said calmly, and nudged a platter full of kelp and krill toward the prisoner. While Silas' nose was down Marianus made his move. He catapulted over the fish, using his tail to backlash Silas' face into the food, before rushing out of the door. Shaking his head to clear his vision of food debris Silas quickly turned to chase the escapee. Exhaling a string of bubbles and curses he charged after Marianus only to bounce back off the door.

"Ha! How do you like it?" Marianus laughed in his face.

"Help! Help!! Triton! Grady! Hale!" Silas called his fellow guards and finally leader. Upon hearing Hale's name Marianus' triumphant grin washed from his face and was replaced by dread. Swimming from the holding area he dashed from one hallway to the next, searching for a way out of the ARK. He saw no one. Not a fish barred his path, not a guard blocked his way. Instead of putting his frantic nerves at ease he started to panic. He swam faster and faster, occasionally bumping into the transparent walls of glass.

On a pass through a deserted corridor he spotted an unmarked canister. It sat atop a quilt covered bed. An unused tank had been turned upside down to cover it, a stack of thick books anchoring it from floating away. Marianus peeked inside the room and was shocked to find it empty. It was too quiet. He could hear the blood rushing in his ears with only the voice of his inner doubt to accompany.

Cautiously he swam into the room and up to the bed to peer at the canister trapped beneath the tank. What else could it be but the changing solution? Altering his plan in the blink of an eye, he decided the solution was coming with him. He gave it a tentative nudge with his nose. The tank remained rooted to its spot. Testing it a bit further he leaned against the tank with his full weight. When he backed away the canister and tank swayed slightly on the coiled bedsprings. Encouraged by the small movement Marianus backed up several feet and swam as hard as he could, barreling into the tank. It rocked precariously on its perch, but did not topple. He repeated his actions again to the same results.

The knowledge of the solution's location alone would not be enough to satisfy Adonis. He must have it. How badly Marianus wanted to be the one to deliver it. Panting and bruised he floated in the doorway readying himself for a final heroic attempt. Using his last reserves of strength he hurtled through the water and into his target. The protective anchor holding down the tank slid from its top and landed on the metal floor with an audible thud. Wasting no time Marianus snatched the canister in his fin and raced back to the cell where Silas was still shouting.

"Where is everyone?" Marianus demanded.

"At a meeting! The same place I was supposed to be after delivering your breakfast."

"Where?"

"Right. Like I'm going to tell you."

"What's this?" Marianus forced another question, and words were not necessary for Marianus know he had guessed correctly. He turned from the cell and boldly swam away, this time toward the center of the ARK instead of its outreaching arms. If they were all gathered in one place at a meeting, there were plenty of places they wouldn't be. Plenty of places where he could escape.

"Wait!" Silas called in despair. But the Admiral was on a mission that would now need a whole lot more than shouting to stop him. Silas watched the blue green splash of color speed away.

Chapter 54
Surface

"He needed something soft and loud and sweet and proud, but tough enough to break a heart, something beautiful, unbreakable that lights up the dark. So God made girls." – from: God Made Girls by Raelynn

Flynn looked over at her brother, his head intently bent over a beaker of neon orange fluid.

"Wicked color choice," she commented.

"We wanted to be able to see it clearly in the water, so we could know, rather than just guess, what it touches and impacts in the ocean," Caspian explained.

"Practical too," Flynn said and moved into take a closer look while he poured the almost fluorescent liquid into small test tubes. He handed each one to her so that she could cover the tubes with a rubber stopper and then set them in a tray. "What's next?" Flynn asked when they had emptied the last of the antidote into the tiny tubes.

"The protein in the antidote needs to cultivate for no less than three point seven five hours. So I'm jobless for a while."

"Me too. Professor Sorenson and Simon had to go to class. They invited me, but I didn't want to miss the delivery."

"I concur," Caspian agreed. "Why don't we head to the TUBE and wait with everyone else?"

"My scientific brain translates that into: let's go hang out by my girlfriend," Flynn teased as the siblings walked from the lab.

"And I suppose you aren't disappointed that Luke will be there as well," Caspian taunted back. Flynn stopped abruptly in the hallway. Her cheeks burning she turned to look at her brother. "What?" he asked. "You aren't the only one on the planet with a license to tease."

"I – I know," she stammered. "I just wasn't sure of it myself, before... before just now, when you called me on it."

"Well it's okay. I mean that you like him. He's a good guy. What's the dilema?"

"I'm just shocked that you noticed. You really have changed," she said taking in all that was Caspian. A smile spread far and wide across her face, but in an instant the corners of her mouth fell and she eyed Caspian critically. "Do you think anyone else knows?"

"Are you kidding me?" Caspian laughed. "I noticed! Of course they all know." Flynn threw her head back and groaned loudly. "Come on Flynn," Caspian said and dragged her down the hallway. Together they walked the halls of the Surface Station loading dock feeling closer than they ever had before.

When they walked into the room they found an entourage of people assembled. Apparently Caspian and Flynn weren't the only ones who didn't want to miss the important delivery. Giving each other knowing smiles they went their separate ways and settled in to wait next to Nina and Luke.

Nina immediately slid her hand into Caspian's as he joined her conversation with a few surface scientists about attending Bay City University next fall. Flynn watched them from where she sat on the floor next to Luke. Caspian caught her eye and gave her a nod of encouragement. She smiled and shook her head at him, but decided to take his advice. Luke's hands rested inside his BCU sweatshirt pocket leaving his elbow easily accessible. Flynn slipped her arm through his and tried hard not to make eye contact with the observant peers that looked her way. For his part Luke didn't skip a beat. Without a pause in his conversation with Pac he leaned his head over to touch hers and a flash of heat spread throughout Flynn's body enflaming her cheeks for the second time in five minutes. *Geez just call me Nina*, Flynn thought. But if she were honest with herself, she couldn't remember when she had ever been happier.

Chapter 55
ARK

"There is a microscopically thin line between being brilliantly creative and acting like the most gigantic idiot on earth. So what the hell, leap." – Cynthia Heimel

Hale had one more task to complete before they all convened. He commandeered a few guards exiting the mess hall and took them with him. By the time they arrived at the TUBE, precious cargo in tow, Aster and her sea stars had already assembled.

"Aster, thank you for coming so quickly. Cover the tube, or as much of it as you can. Sneak out through any opening in the bubble you can find and place yourselves along this glass. From the sea floor to the surface, it is your job to protect the TUBE. Do not let anyone see inside. Do not let any creature break through. We must protect what is inside at all costs."

"You can count on us," Aster assured. Like tiny spiders crawling across an invisible web, the starfish separated across the water and then joined again. Placing themselves one next to the other, interlocking their colorful arms, they covered the glass. A protective layer grew from the bottom up, stretching to the surface. When the rest of the allies arrived, their wall had grown so high that Hale could no longer see open ocean through the tunnel of the TUBE. He turned his back on Aster's progress and searched the crowd for Silas' face. He would have rather seen him here before continuing, seen his steady nod to know the job was done, but they could not wait any longer. He would have to trust in the fish, just as Hale had asked of him. He took a deep breath and addressed the assembled allies.

"Allies, minutes ago, the prisoner Marianus escaped." Gasps echoed throughout the loading dock. Hale hushed them and then continued. "He thinks he is taking with him a supply of changing solution." Cries of outrage bounced off the walls now and it took much longer for Hale to quiet them this time. "Do not worry. It is all a part of the plan. I am telling you these things because I want there to be no secrets between us. Secrets led Dathan to a watery grave. I do not want to repeat his mistakes. We are all in this together and everyone must know." The tension in the small space was thick, but at last the allies were quiet. "We have let him escape. Let him think he has stolen that which his master most desires. What he has taken is a jar full of colored sea water. Nothing more. Let him think they've tricked us. Over-confidence is a curse, a curse that could be their undoing. It is our hope that Marianus will rush to Adonis with this pseudo-solution, tying up his attention for a short time, allowing us to transfer the real supply of the changing solution to the surface, forever out of our enemy's fins." At this Hale unveiled the real supply of PE-328 he had brought with him and the allies cheered. Hale let them.

Chapter 56
Underwater Cave

"If you can find a path with no obstacles, it probably doesn't lead anywhere." – Frank A. Clark

Marianus swam faster than he ever had before. Even with the cumbersome canister tucked under his fin, he sped through the water making good time. He was being followed. He knew it. But he also knew that if he made it back into Water Warrior territory before they caught up to him, he was as good as home.

He flipped his fins, propelling himself forward as fast as possible. His front fins burned as they grasped the solution. It kept sliding, slipping. *Hang on*, he told himself. *You're almost there.* But try as he might, he could not hold it. It fell to the sea floor, landing and creating a plume of fine sand. When the water cleared he swooped down to gather it again.

It was then the shadow passed over head, forcing his body to seize with fear. When Marianus looked up, he almost wished it was the barracuda guard's eyes that stared back at him. Or the jellyfish's. Even Hale's. He wished it was anybody but the fearsome figure that hovered in front of him.

"Thank goodness someone else in this operation has some brains. If I had left things entirely up to that fool Adonis, we'd all be sitting pretty on a seafood platter by now."

"Marianus bit back a defense for his beloved leader and instead merely nodded.

"I have done what I need to do and will now escort you home like the hero you are. Here, let me carry that for you," she said reaching out a tentacle and relieving Marianus of his package.

Together they swam back to the underwater cave in

silence. Shortly before arriving, Marianus' companion returned the canister to him and ordered him to tell no one of their encounter. He watched dazed and exhausted as his worst nightmare swam to another cave entrance, leaving him alone, a quarter of a mile separating him and the glory of delivering the changing solution to Adonis.

He charged up to the shark guards blocking the entrance to the cave and without a word they let him in. Marianus was relieved to find Adonis in the great room of the cave. He wasn't sure if he could swim a foot farther.

Adonis was mid meal, surrounded by Water Warriors, but talking to none of them. His thoughts were obviously occupied on something other than small talk. When he saw Marianus he abandoned his food and his meal companions and raced to his side. Marianus' heart swelled with pride.

"I have it. The changing solution! I've done it Sir!" Marianus boasted between his ragged breaths and thrust the canister into Adonis' fins.

"Well done Marianus! Well done!" Adonis turned from his loyal servant and swam quickly to the front of the cave. "Warriors! This is a blessed morning! Today, because of the cunning and bravery of Admiral Marianus, we are a league closer to our destiny!" The dining creatures stopped eating to listen and watch while Adonis raved about his star soldier. Marianus, standing next to him, positively glowed in his praise. "I hold here a container of the changing solution. I hold the power to control the ocean. I hold the answer to our revenge against the humans' for destroying our underwater world. I hold the power to end them."

At the conclusion of his tirade he motioned to the back of the room. A pair of guards ducked into the maze of caves and a short time later returned with a lone prisoner in tow. It was easy to see from the creature's vacant expression that this was a creature unchanged. No confusion crossed its face, no thoughts were plainly written in its eyes. It remained just a crab, a 10 armed, blue shelled, beautifully dangerous crab. Marianus had never seen a crab like this before. It was small in comparison to some of the creatures gathered, but large for a crab. His body was almost 10 inches across, not counting the extension of its dangerous pincher clad arms. Adonis must have sent someone as far as the Gulf of Mexico to find such a specimen. And now, this creature would be on their team, their side, their warrior.

"Warriors!" Adonis addressed them. "Meet our newest recruit, the Beauty Blue Crab. There are hundreds more just like him in the caves behind you, just itching to take their revenge on the humans. These beauties have been hunted for years by the land walkers for the sweet and succulent meat that lies beneath their gorgeous blue shell. With them, our army will grow only stronger and when we meet with the ARK allies and the humans, it will be with the help of their decimating pincers that we succeed. Shall we meet our new hero?" The warriors cheered and shouted, urging their leader on. A chant began to grow.

"Change! Change! Change!" Amidst the roar of the crowd the crab tried to scuttle away, its claws scrabbling on the rocky floor of the cave, but the guards encircled around him left him no room to escape. Adonis dramatically raised the canister and poured the green liquid out onto the blue beauty, baptizing him into the brotherhood of the Water Warriors. As the solution touched the shell of the crab the room silenced and everyone watched and waited to see the transformation. But nothing happened. The crab remained mute and huddled on the floor. Adonis reached out a fin to poke the creature, prompting it to utter even a single syllable, but instead of the satisfaction he had been searching for, the crab snapped at his fin. A single stream of blood siphoned into the water.

Complete and utter bedlam filled the cave. Adonis viciously attacked the crab with his tail, flicking it into the wall of the cave. Its shell crunched audibly and more dolphins immediately picked up where Adonis left off, battering the blue shelled beauty until white flesh poked out from under its protective layer. Adonis wheeled on Marianus, insults and curses flowing faster than a waterfall.

"You fool! This was a decoy! This was nothing! How could you be so stupid?!" Marianus' dreams and heart shattered with each verbal assault. He backed into a corner covering as much of his face with his fins as possible so Adonis would not see him cry.

The sharks, blood lust in their noses, needed to be held back. Their natural instincts were stronger than their human intelligence at this moment and despite the ring of protection surrounding Adonis as he berated Marianus, they circled, intent on satisfying their craving.

A single voice and presence stilled them all.
"Enough!!!!"
Adonis stopped yelling. Marianus stopped crying. The sharks stopped circling and everyone looked to the gigantic form filling the room at the edge of the labyrinth. Only the water current moved as they took in the beast before them.

"You will do as I say," the creature began. "If this is not the changing solution," it said gesturing with a long tentacle, "then the real supply must still be out there. Go. Get it. Bring it here and we will carry on with our plan." The creatures gathered, too fearful to make any noise, only nodded. "Do not fail me." The threat was clear, despite the lack of specification.

They rushed from the cave, whether eager to act, or for fear of their lives, it did not matter. They swam without formation, without order, a single purpose on their mind. The Water Warriors were a giant cloud of fury and fear. They were going to the ARK to get the solution one way or another. They would not fail this time. Could not.

Chapter 57
Surface

"Success isn't permanent and failure isn't fatal." – Mike Ditka

"I can't stand this waiting anymore!" Sonora whined. Murmurs of agreement around the room echoed her thoughts. "I wish there was a way to know what was going on down there."

"Oh my gosh! There is!" Flynn said jumping up, almost toppling Luke over as she did so. "I don't know why we didn't think of it before!" She dashed from the room, leaving the rest of her comrades speechless and confused. A minute later she returned with Simon's remote controlled fish-cam in hands. "We can use this to check things out, see what's happening!"

"Flynn, you are brilliant!" Caspian exclaimed.

"It's not my fault you all overlook the most obvious solution and leave me to save the day," she responded smiling.

"You will also be a dead brilliant scientist if you send that off without me," Simon teased as he walked into the room. Removing Nora's less than favorite pompon clad hat, he tossed it on his desk and then took up a position on his knees next to Flynn at the top of the Tube.

"Of course," Flynn said magnanimously handing over the device. Simon took the fish from her outstretched hands, flipped the on switch and placed it gently in the water. Flynn opened a software window on Simon's desktop computer and within a minute, the entire room was on a virtual field trip to the ARK.

"It's darker than I remember," Nina commented. "It's the middle of the day. Why isn't it brighter in the TUBE?"

"Look here," Simon pointed out as he swam closer to the wall of the TUBE. A vision of starfish undercarriages filled the computer screen. "They must be trying to cover up the TUBE. Protect it maybe, or cover up what is going on inside."

"Man, those are some smart fish!" Pac praised.

"Indeed they are," Mr. Brinestone agreed.

For several more minutes the scientists watched as Simon maneuvered the fish down the TUBE to the ARK. The scenery didn't change much, but still their eyes were glued to the screen, not wanting to miss a single second of the footage. They were so engrossed they didn't see or hear Professor Sorenson come in.

"Well, while the cat's away the mice will play!" he said jovially. "Who said you could do anything exciting without me?" he teased.

"Sorry Professor," Flynn said with a sheepish smile.

"It's alright. You're forgiven. If I'm not mistaken, we are almost there, so I didn't miss anything really. Simon, don't forget to turn on the audio capabilities."

Simon flipped a switch on his remote control just as the loading dock came into view. Now they could both see and hear as Hale directed Jett to enter the TUBE.

"Swim straight up Jett. The humans should be waiting for you. Make sure that they get the delivery, but careful not to touch them. Don't leave immediately. Wait to see if they have any messages for you to bring back down. Then, swim back the way you came. Hopefully you'll be able to get back before the Water Warriors even know you left."

"Got it," Jett nodded. "And no worries Hale. This will be a piece of cake."

"Cake?" Hale asked confused.

"Nevermind," Jett said and in true teenager fashion rolled his eyes.

"Swim Safe Jett," Hale concluded.

"Swim strong."

Jett wrapped his tentacles around the canister and lifted it from the metal grated floor. He lifted it up above his head and the Allies cheered once more, sending him off with hope and happiness. Ducking into the TUBE he glanced up toward the surface and came face to face with the fish-cam.

"Well hello there little guy! How did you get in here?" Jett asked.

"Jett!" Stillman said comandeering the microphone imbedded in the fish. "It's us, I mean me! Stillman-

"and Sonora!" came a shout from the back of the room.

"This is a fish-cam," Stillman explained as he sat next to Simon. "We came to check on you."

"Sweet, now I'll have a travel companion. But we better get going. Hale is nervous the Water Warriors are on their way."

As he swam upward, Jett told the scientists all that had happened below the surface that morning. It was an enthusiastic tale, one Jett enjoyed telling as much as the humans enjoyed hearing it. And like any story, it passed the time quickly. They were less than 100 feet from the surface when a stream of daylight shone into the TUBE, momentarily blinding the swimmers.

"They're coming!" a single starfish shouted.

"How many?" Jett asked.

"All of them!" the starfish responded frantically.

"All of the dolphins? All of the sharks?"

"Dolphins, sharks, Mahi… ALL OF THEM!"

"Sea silt and foam froth," Jett swore.

"Swim!!" Stillman shouted.

Speed had never been one of Jett's strong suits, but he moved as fast as his undulating body would allow. The fish-cam sped ahead of him, not wanting to get in the way. It half flew out of the water and into Simon's outstretched hands. He bundled his scientific baby in his sweatshirt and then moved out of the way to make room for Professor Sorenson and Dr.

Brinestone. Together they peered over the edge of the TUBE into the water. Sleeves rolled up they readied themselves to pull the canister up and of the water.

Bass reverberations could be heard from far below and the surface of the water inside the TUBE shook with little tremors. The Water Warriors were trying to break through the tube. The starfish held strong, their bristly bodies protecting the water highway connecting the ARK and the surface.

When Jett came into view the two grown men thrust their hands into the water and reached out for the container of changing solution. Attempting to avoid the perilous tentacles of the jellyfish, they stretched to grasp their goal. They were so close.

Meaty Mahi heads and powerful dolphin tails thrashed against the echinoderm encrusted TUBE. Shark snouts repeatedly bashed against the creatures and fiberglass. The starfish did all they could, giving Jett more time that he otherwise would have had, but in the end, the beating was too much and the Water Warriors broke through the TUBE.

Bits of broken sea star bodies and shards of glass exploded in all directions. Dr. Brinestone screamed in agony as a piece of the TUBE impaled his right arm. Blood flowed freely from his arm into the water, attracting the attention of the already blood thirsty sharks.

"Get him out of here!" Professor Sorenson yelled. "And get me a net!" With a flurry of activity they complied with his requests. The close quarters of the loading dock and Simon's desk made following his orders difficult, but they managed all the same. Despite his protests to continue helping, Dr. Brinestone was dragged to a hallway where 911 was called and Mrs. Brinestone began administering first aid. A net was brought forward and in one quick swoop Jett was lifted from the TUBE, canister and all.

"Quick! To a salt water tank!" Sonora shouted as she moved with Professor Sorenson and his load down a hall.

Stillman, and several surface scientists followed, passing the reclined and bloody form of Dr. Brinestone as he lay on the floor.

"Someone grab that canister and check its sustainability! Make sure to store it at 45 degrees Fahrenheit or it will lose it's-"

"Enough already!" Mrs. Brinestone cut off her husband. "Let someone who hasn't severed a major artery take care of it."

Mr. Brinestone groaned, whether from frustration or from the pain induced my Mrs. Brinestone's pressure applying hands was uncertain. Seconds later his eyes rolled in the back of his head and he passed out. Mrs. Brinestone called for help and several more scientists rushed to her aid. Together they maneuvered him up into their collective arms and carried him to a place within the station where the ambulance would be able to more easily access him. Once they were down the hall and eerie silence filled the loading dock. Only the sound of water sloshing out of the TUBE's gaping mouth filled the once full and noisy room.

"Simon!" Flynn shouted, "Quick! The fish-cam! Get it back in the water. We have to know what is happening!"

With a splash the fish-cam was back in the water, swimming and swerving to avoid collision with the chaos that reigned below. TUBE debris and fins and oxygen bubbles filled the water making it hard for the camera to make sense of the scene. Some eyes were glued to the screen while a few more hovered over the edge of the broken TUBE attempting to gauge the action from above.

Details were not precise, but it looked like the starfish had abandoned their station on the TUBE and reformed at the opening of the ARK loading dock. Several layers thick in that concentrated space, their tiny pink and orange bodies created an impenetrable wall, preventing any of the Water Warriors from entering the ARK. The scientists continued to watch, their rapidly beating hearts ready to burst with anxiety.

"What do we do now?" Flynn asked.

"We're going in," Caspian said authoritatively.

"Now?" Nina asked.

"Yes, now," Caspian said. "We're alone. No one can stop us." Nina looked around the room and then truth of his words sunk in. Besides herself and Caspian, only Simon, Flynn, Luke and Pac remained in the room. Everyone else had gone off to see Jett safely into a tank, check the returned supply of PE-328 or assist Mrs. Brinestone with her injured husband.

"I like where you're head's at," Pac said, his typically mischievous smile plastered clear across his face.

"You heard the man," Luke said standing next to his best friend. "Suit up."

"I'm sorry to rain on your parade," Professor Bebee apologized as she reentered the room. "But that is absolutely not going to happen."

Chapter 58
Underwater Cave

"The struggle you're in today is developing the strength you need for tomorrow." – Robert Tew

Blood in the water. So much blood.

The sharks circled, snapping their jaws, snatching a bite of a dolphin here and a tuna there. It had been so long since they'd had a decent meal and the fresh flesh tasted so good. For seemingly endless minutes, terror and chaos reigned beneath the water. Adonis and Marianus rushed from warrior to warrior begging them to calm down and come to their senses. But they wouldn't listen. Their natural instincts, fight, flight, eat, survive were in total command.

The tornado of destruction spread out from the vortex that was the TUBE. Glass, blood, fish, dicension, sharks, rage, debris, helplessness, fury… out and out it spiraled until finally it dissipated leaving behind visible signs of destruction and only the smell of blood in the water.

When their human cognition returned to the forefront of their brains, guilt washed over the sharks. They hung their heads in the presence of the few warriors close enough to make eye contact. Their full bellies taunted their conscience and more than a few wretched up what used to be their fellow comrades.

Not knowing what else to do, those who remained alive soberly swam back to the cave. They gathered at the entrance waiting for their commanders to enter, but they hesitated as well. Only when Adonis arrived did they stumble into the cave.

She was waiting for them in the place where Adonis usually spoke. She looked ready to address them now and so they filed in, formed a loose version of their ranks, ready to listen. Expecting to be, at the very least, severely scolded, they were shocked when the beast before them spoke gently, even motherly.

"My poor darlings. What an awful day for you. I never would have sent you if I had known. But don't worry. We'll do better next time." She looked at them and sensed they did not want there to be a next time. But there would be. She would not rest until this war was won and the humans had paid for their mistakes. They just needed to wait for the right time. She needed time.

Across the ocean another gathering was taking place. Behind the solid starfish barricade the Allies discussed their next move. This way of life could not continue. Now, at least, the changing solution was safely out of the water. But what next?

Each member of the council voiced the opinions of their fellow creatures while Hale and the rest of the Allies listened. Wait for the humans to make a plan. Swim far, far away. Find a new safer headquarters. Launch a sneak attack. Many options swirled around in the heads of the Allies, but no one knew which one to pick.

Above them all, the scientists worked diligently. They checked the antidote hourly. They checked its composition against the liquid that had gotten them all into this mess. They theorized, calculated, observed and analyzed. Finally, long after the sun had gone down, they had achieved success in the state of ten mini vials of PE-328 antidote. But ten vials was not enough for success. Ten vials was not enough to solve the problems of an entire ocean.

Not caring for the hour of the clock, they worked on, duplicating their process, knowing that the creation of more antidote was imperative to their mission.

Calculate. Observe. Analyze. Repeat.

When the sun rose, the scientists looked with bleary

eyes on gallons of potential antidote filling every available counter space. In 3.75 hours, according to Caspian's calculations, the proteins would be calibrated and the antidote would be ready to work. Not bothering to drive home, they found a couch or chair or small stretch of carpet and collapsed with exhaustion into a deep, deep sleep.

    Simon found them there after his early morning lecture class. Propped up next to his desk was a note.

Ready to roll. Antidote creation complete. Let the little dudes below know we plan to meet them at the Outlier Station at noon. We end this thing today.

— Luke

    Wasting no time, Simon quickly readied the fish-cam and released it into the water. He swam straight for the pink and orange bull's eye on the ocean floor that was the starfish wall of protection. A patrol fish picked him up immediately and swam with him the rest of the way. Simon relayed the scientists' message and then waited while Hale communicated it to the rest of the Allies. A vote was proposed, taken and passes. They were all in.

    Simon hightailed it the way he came wondering if the end was really in sight.

Chapter 59
Surface

"What is the use in living if not to strive for nobel causes and to make this muddled world a better place for those who will live in it after you are gone." – Winston Churchill

While they had been creating the antidote, Simon had apparently been doing more than going to class. A selection of single frame shots collected from his fish-cam were spread out across an unrolled map that covered the entire surface of the table. Through them they had learned that Adonis and his Water Warriors were coming and going from a large sea cave. The location of their no longer secret headquarters was 5 miles north, just off the coast. The crew sat gathered around a large table in the Surface Station. Conversation echoed off of the metal walls and furniture fixtures as they made their plan.

The Allies planned to meet them at the Outlier Station in just a few hours and so much had to be done before then. But none of it could be accomplished before the crew was selected. Caspian argued vehemently that leaving the children behind last time had been a huge mistake. Stillman added that the teens' relationship with the ARK Allied forces was much stronger than the still fresh relationship the adults had fostered with the creatures. The adults, as always, argued with the chief concerns of safety and wisdom.

Nora and Simon sat back and watched the superb show of brain power duke it out across the table. On one side Caspian, Flynn, and Stillman put up an aggressive front while on the opposite side of the table both professors and Mrs. Brinestone matched them point for point. Dr. Brinestone recently released from the hospital sat silently, his eyes volleying back and forth between discussion points.

"Who's your money on?" Nora whispered to Simon.

"I don't know. Professor Sorenson is looking solid, but that Flynn girl is pretty feisty."

"She's my girl and my money's on her," Nora smiled at him. Simon stretched out his hand and when she shook it he said,

"Loser buys ice cream."

"Like on a date?" Nora's eyebrows arched up into her forehead.

"Yup," Simon said confidently. Nora took her time answering, appraising Simon's honest face, goofy hat and open smile.

"You're on," Nora said with a firm shake.

Dr. Brinestone, still grievously wounded, was definitely not up for the mission. Sonora also chose to bow out saying she was just too scared to go back. No one blamed her. The surface scientists felt out of their league, their land legs useless in the wide open ocean. Noah was at school and unable to cast his own vote, but his parents crossed him off the list of candidates almost immediately. Pac had promised Noah just that morning that he wouldn't do anything cool without him. He regretted that promise now, but tracking down a psycho dolphin on a power trip did register pretty high on the coolness-scale, so he would stay behind and keep Noah company. It was decided, and said as nicely as possible, that Nina's newness to the underwater world made her a larger liability than asset. Even though she was disappointed, she said she understood, and was embarrassed to find herself more relieved than anything. Professor Bebee also decided to stay at the Surface Station and monitor from above. Simon would give his right eye to go, but his aptitude for a joystick and knowledge of the fish-cam required him to stay behind as well.

Little by little their list dwindled down until only a few names remained. In the end, Simon had a debt to pay, because in just a few hours, Mrs. Brinestone, Professor Sorenson, both older Brinestone children, Stillman, Luke and Anton would be heading into Adonis' lair.

Chapter 60
Outlier Station

"What we do in life, echoes in all of eternity." – from: Gladiator (the movie)

"We are an unlikely army of heroes. We are the small of the ocean, but we are not weak. And we will not cower in the face of the brutes we go against. Our courage and our cause make us mighty. And we will win," Hale rallied. His words punctuated the tense atmosphere and charged the allies before him with electric enthusiasm. The humans listened from within the Outlier Station, equally as entranced by the small but charismatic leader. "We are done waiting for these monsters to make their move. Today we will make our stand together," Hale gestured to the assembled allies and to the humans inside the small bubble, "Together we will overcome our foe and stop them from destroying this world."

Silently Jett wondered, *and then what?* But there was no time for Hale to answer. It was time to answer the battle call and Jett would rather be skewered and served for dinner than miss it. Following his rank of jellyfish he fell in line and moved forward. He was grateful Stillman had insisted on bringing him back to his natural habitat, rather than have been left behind in the sterile Surface Station alone, worried and bored.

The humans quickly loaded their submarine and joined the procession. What a sight they all made. Jellyfish, turtles, angelfish, sea snakes, starfish and more. An unlikely army of heroes Hale had called them. Their unlikely, small, fail bodies amassed to form a cloud of courage ready to take over the sea. They were ready.

It took quite a while for the army to travel the four

miles from the Outlier Station to the cave. When they arrived they found the Water Warriors similarly assembled outside of the entrance to Adonis' headquarter. How they knew the Allies and the humans were coming was a mystery, but there assemblage did not change their plans. If anything it made it easier.

As Flynn suited up with her SCUBA gear inside the sub her scientific mind tried to count the bodies she saw lined up outside the window and when that failed, she tried to calculate. Row upon row, of creatures spread out before the cave. The ARK Allies floated on one side, the Water Warriors on the other. The commanders stood at attention, the first in each line. The humans, once outside of the sub, were placed precariously in the middle. As if by silent command, the commanders swam forward to greet the humans and each other.

A turtle, barracuda, sea snake, starfish, jellyfish, angelfish, dolphin, shark, Mahi, and 7 humans gathered in the unmarked neutral territory at the center of the gathering. Luke thought it sounded like the start of a good joke, but was sure at this moment it would not be well received. Instead he said,

"We end this today."

"Oh, you're done destroying the planet are you?" Adonis said mockingly. "Thank you for the advanced notice."

"Sarcasm will not solve this problem," Caspian replied.

"I know, but it makes me happy. The fact that it annoys you is just a pleasant side effect," Adonis chided.

"Enough," Mrs. Brinestone said eyeing them both with a motherly stare. "Dolphin,"

"Adonis,"

"Whatever," Mrs. Brinestone spat back, issuing a huge grin from her daughter. "We apologize for the inconvenience our experiment has caused you. We plan to right the situation as soon as possible. We are coming here today to ask for your cooperation in the process. The antidote is ready. We need only to test it and then we will begin administering it to you all."

"Yeah, that's not really going to work for us. See, we have other plans," Adonis said casually.

"What plans?" Anton demanded.

"Spreading the change across the oceans," Adonis began, his voice hardening with every word spoken. "Convincing all the sea creatures to join our cause. Avoiding the nets of fishermen and starving the planet. We want revenge for all of the inconveniences you humans have caused. We will take control and we will end you."

"We meant you no harm!" Professor Sorenson boomed. "If anything we were trying to help!"

"Good intentions aside, you have made quite a mess of things, and we intend to do the same," Adonis carried on, seemingly oblivious to their fury.

"What's with this 'we' crap? Have you told your underlings this plan? They look a little undecided. I dare say their touch of humanness allowed them to develop a conscience!" Flynn spat every word with venom, covering her facemask with spit and hoping to inspire rebellion in the creatures surrounding their summit.

"They will do what I say!" Adonis snapped. Momentarily drawn into the verbal assaults, he darted forward to stare Flynn down. Their noses almost touched as they met eye to dagger throwing eye.

"Are you so sure?" Flynn unflinchingly asked back.

Indeed the commanders began to look around, uneasy with the new direction the war had taken in the last few hours.

"This has gone on long enough," Luke said hoisting the harpoon. Steadying the weapon on his shoulder he winked through the scope and lined up his shot. "Clear!" he shouted and then fired.

As the barbed spear sliced through the water, both the

humans and the animal commanders backed away from Adonis. All except for one. Marianus darted forward, attempting to shield his beloved leader. The sharp point shot clean through his body and he was instantly dead. His body hung from the line trailing back to Luke. The spear, shot at close range, continued through and met its intended mark, pinning Adonis to the outer wall of the cave. After a stunned moment of silence, Professor Sorenson and his crew swam forward. Seeing the commanders stunned to stillness, they felt brave enough to approach Adonis' struggling form.

A gurgling laugh escaped Adonis' lips mingling with the blood in the water.

"What's so funny?" Luke spat from behind the harpoon.

"You think you've won."

"We have! We defeated you. Your lungs have been pierced. They are filling with blood and sea water as we speak. You have minutes left to live if you're lucky," Anton explained in a hate-laced voice.

"You're right. I am lucky. Because I am going to die."

"Then what was all this about?" Flynn questioned, waving her arms gesturing to his army.

"I'm not the bad guy you're looking for. I was only a distraction. A puppet. The one you really have to worry about is still out there."

"Tell us!" shouted Luke.

"Her name is Nycho Teuthis," Adonis nearly whispered. "And you can find her, in there," He pointed with his fin to the depths of the cave that had been his headquarters. His final act of betrayal complete, Adonis closed his eyes, exhaled his remaining breath, sagged against the wall and died.

"Ny-ko Toothless?" Luke asked, a confused look upon his face.

"Nycho Tuethis," Professor Solomon corrected.

"Whatever she is, Nycho sounds psycho," Flynn stated.

"With a name like that, it can only be one creature," Stillman said.

"What?" Flynn asked.

"The colossal squid," answered professor Sorenson and Caspian in unison.

Chapter 61
Underwater Cave

"'We'll be friends forever won't we Pooh?' Piglet asked. 'Even longer,' Pooh answered." – A.A. Milne

Without Adonis to lead them and Marianus dead as well, the Water Warriors became curiously subdued. It didn't take much to choral them and then keep them complacently in place with a ring of jellyfish.

"Let's tackle one problem at a time," Professor Sorenson said as he directed Mrs. Brinestone and the children to reenter the submarines. He turned to Hale and asked, "Can you keep these urchins under control until we return?"

"Absolutely," Hale assured.

"Excellent. We will go back to the surface. Assess the quality of our antidote and come back as quickly as possible to set things back to normal." Hale nodded his understanding and Professor Sorenson swam back to the sub to rejoin his crew. Just meters from the submarine hatch Jett stopped the professor.

"Sir, if I may, can I suggest two willing participants to test the antidote?" he asked.

"Of course! In fact, it would be wonderful to have volunteers."

"Great. Expect two jellyfish to arrive at what's left of the Surface Station loading dock in a few hours. They'll be there," Jett promised.

Once inside the submarine and dry, the humans checked on the Allies' firm hold over the Water Warriors before heading back to the Surface Station. As they departed the adults busied themselves with traveling tasks and discussions about the antidote preparations and administration processes. Caspian, Flynn, Stillman, Luke and Anton remained next to the windows, looking back at the friends they continued to leave behind again and again.

Jett watched the submarine until it was out of sight and then returned to the cave where the sea snakes and jellyfish had made a double wall of protection around the Water Warriors. Many of the prisoners hovered barely above the sea floor, floating in stunned silence and confusion. The barracuda's worked to free Adonis from the wall and bury him next to a mound of sand and stones that Jett assumed entombed Marianus.

After a brief conversation, Hale granted him permission to return to the ARK. Jett paused to take in the scene of his friends working side by side to complete the tasks that must be done. His heart hurt to know that in a few hours their friendships would be undone, that after all they had been through together none of them would remember an instant of it once the antidote touched their skin. With a huge sigh he turned his back on them and began the long journey to his parents. He battled mixed emotions in his head and heart. Relief for his parents, sadness of his own, uncertainty in it all. What was the right thing to do in this situation? What there a right path to take? He didn't get far before a familiar voice shouted to him, interrupting his thoughts and his progress forward.

"Leaving without a goodbye old friend?" 'Cuda asked him.

"I was hoping if I didn't say it out loud it wouldn't be true," Jett confessed.

"You don't know that this is the last time we'll see each other... like this," 'Cuda finished less confidently than he intended.

"You're right," Jett said, "But I also don't know that it isn't." 'Cuda had no words for him. He nodded stoically, wishing he could give his friend a hug, or even a fin-bump.

But fear of bodily harm made him keep his distance. Jett understood and wished for the thousandth time that things didn't have to change.

"I'll be back after I get my parents to the Surface Station. I might be back before the change," Jett said.

"Swim safe," 'Cuda said.

"Swim strong," Jett finished.

Chapter 62
Surface

"Persistence propels potential to perfection." – *Soichiro Honda*

When the submarines arrived back at the surface, the station was whipped into a full blown tornado of action. Gear was unloaded from the sub only to be restocked with fresh supplies. The antidote was checked and a tank was prepared for the arrival of the test subjects. The rest of the valuable liquid was packed for travel and placed carefully inside the sub. Professor Sorenson ordered scientists around as expertly as a commander instructs his troops. Mrs. Brinestone relayed the entire adventure to her husband who was dismayed to have missed all the action. Amidst the storm, the junior memebers of the crew sat moping, a center of calm.

When the jellyfish did arrive, the loading dock area went from standing room only to a ghost town. Sonora couldn't bring herself to watch them change and when she refused to follow Steve and Adriel down the hallway, the others stayed behind as well, so that only the children remained. Caspian tried to convince them that this was the right thing to do scientifically. That whether they meant to or not, the animals would wreak undoable damage on the ocean if they left them this way, but not even he fell for his own pep talk. Nora found them this way, leaning against lab tables and huddled in dramatic poses of despair.

"I took the boys shopping," Nora said taking a seat next to Flynn and Luke.

"Really?" Flynn asked. "I'm not sure even shopping would cheer me up right now."

"Never underestimate the power of retail therapy," Nora said. With a smile she grandly gestured to the doorway as Pac and Noah walked in sporting gigantic plastic squirt guns complete with backpack reserve tanks.

"If we gotta do this at least we can have a little fun," Pac said pretended to blast them all with his new toys. When they didn't move or even smile Pac continued, "C'mon, you guys. Luke, I know you, you're dying to get your hands on this." He walked to his friend and forced him to grudgingly put on his own set of water battle gear pulled from one of Nora's many shopping bags.

"You know," Luke said smiling. "This gives me an idea."

"I love your ideas," Pac said pleased he'd cheered up his friend.

"Well, all of you are gonna love this one. Everybody in, we don't have long. Simon and Nora, get in here too, we're going to need everyone if this is going to work."

The kids huddled around Luke as he explained his plan. It didn't take long for them to all buy in. Arms waved frantically, volunteering for jobs as plans were urgently whispered. Someone dug out a map while Flynn rummaged through drawers looking for a subsea compass. Stillman expertly surfed the internet brushing up on his aquatic animal facts as Sonora and Nina referenced similar material in their sea guides. Luke polished his harpoon while Caspian and Simon coordinated their separate missions to eventually combine into one overall master plan. When the adults were ready to leave an hour later, so were they.

"Alright load up everyone!" Mrs. Brinestone said as calmly as if she were telling them all to get into a minivan and head to a soccer tournament. As all of the kids moved to get in the sub she said, "Hold up now, what's going on here? We don't have room for everybody."

"I can stay behind," Nina volunteered. Simon and Nora echoed her with a "me too."

"There's still too many," Mrs. Brinestone said sadly.

"Mom," Noah began. "These are our friends. Can you at least let us say goodbye?"

"Alright," she said after a moment, "I suppose we can make that work. Alright people, prepare the second sub."

"No need Mrs. B. We got that covered while you guys were testing the antidote," Luke said.

Mrs. Brinestone nodded her understanding and approval at their ability to think ahead. "Okay then, like I said, load up!" As they moved to board the subs Luke caught Flynn's eye and winked. She shook her head at this poor romantic timing but couldn't help smiling anyway.

Fully loaded with people and supplies the submarines pulled away from the Surface Station and began heading back to the cave. Everyone inside was intent on completing their mission. Too bad it wasn't the same one.

Chapter 63
Underwater Cave

"And that is how change happens. One gesture. One person. One moment at a time." – from: The Sweet Far Thing by Libba Bray

It was nearing last light when the submarines pulled up to the cave. Already their headlights were on, covering the gathered creatures in a golden glow. A number of the scientists exited the submarine, including the five children from the morning's mission and the additional member of Pac.

The adults had agreed to let Caspian say something to the entire group, before they would start administering the antidote. Flynn was jealous of Caspian for quite a bit of his life, but she did not envy him in this moment.

"Friends," he started. "That's what we are. Friends. I want you to know that we," he gestured to the humans both in the water and in the sub, "have always done our best to protect you. To fight for you, both before the change and after. We have always done what we thought was best, what we thought was right. I know we have made some mistakes and for that we are truly sorry. We are here today to change you back." His voice faltered and he had to choke back a lump in his throat. He would have been embarrassed, but as he looked around, he saw Flynn's tears were freely flowing and Sonora up in the submarine was a legitimate dam broken open to tears. "We think it is best to return you to your natural form. We will never forget you." He locked eyes with 'Cuda. "Never."

'Cuda swam forward and touched the tip of his nose to Caspian's forehead. At this display Kurma, a recently returned Jett, and even Pelamis swam to him and repeated the gesture. The rest of the children flocked to the gathering and said their own goodbyes. Hugs and tears and whispers exchanged fiercely between the sea creatures and humans. Sonora pressed her hand to the glass and they each in turn touched the transparent glass beneath her palm. Noah stood next to her and waved to each creature as it passed the window. They each gave him their best version of a thumbs up before returning to their position among the sea creatures. The adults looked on in wonder, knowing that the animals weren't the only ones to emerge from this catastrophe changed.

    Mrs. Brinestone swam to an open place in the sea between the humans and the creatures and explained that once the antidote touched their skin, the animals would return to their natural state within a minute or two. It had taken less than 45 seconds on their test subjects in the Surface Station. This meant that there was little time for them to depart the scene before their natural instincts would again take over. In less than a minute predators would hunt again and prey would be eaten. In less than a minute they would turn from allies to enemies. But they were not to worry. They would proceed systematically, starting with the smallest, most defenseless creatures, giving them plenty of time to retreat before the larger animals again became hunters. The angelfish would go first and the sea snakes last. Over the course of the next weeks and months, the antidote would be released into the waters of the surrounding area, putting any creature not present, back to their natural state. Eventually, everything would be back to normal.

    At the end of her explanation, the humans began an organized division of the animals into groups by their kind. As a parade of animals filed off into separate groups, congestion first filled the area outside the cave, but with the humans directing traffic, it became an orderly organization quickly.

The two subs circled the perimeter of the area, ready to chase down any escapees, but the animals put up little to no resistance to the humans herding and reigning. As sad as some of the animals seemed, most appeared ready for this madness to end. Only the jellyfish remained separated, floating in a restraining ring around both the herd of dolphins and school of sharks. It appeared as if everyone was compliant, but the scientists didn't want to take any chances, especially when they were so close to ending this catastrophe. As Mrs. Brinestone explained, the angelfish went first. The giant squirt guns simultaneously sprayed the colorful fish, filling the water with the neon colored antidote. Silence permeated the water, humans and animals alike holding their breath awaiting the impact and results.

The orange liquid hung suspended for a few seconds before descending on the gathering of fish. As it fell on them the fish couldn't help but flinch. They couldn't remember if the change had hurt last time, but their fear was unnecessary. The antidote washed over their beautiful scales without inducing an ounce of pain. As the antidote took hold on their bodies and began to work its scientific wonders, the fish visibly relaxed. Their faces went from concerned to peaceful and when the transformation was complete their expressions were startled, but otherwise blank. The humans encircling them broke apart leaving them an available exit out toward the open ocean. Flynn swam up behind them, gently moving them along, toward safety and freedom.

The process took much longer than the scientists anticipated. The change happened quickly enough, but convincing the animals to flee the area was a little more challenging. They spent many minutes after each transformation shooing the creatures out and away from the cave. After the angelfish, turtles, Mahi and dolphins had been changed, the humans re-boarded the submarines to fill their oxygen tanks and restock their supply of antidote.

"Are we really going to do this?" Stillman asked Caspian as they both bent over to refill an oxygen tank, the rush of the air, concealing their whispered exchange.

"Absolutely," Caspian responded seriously. After refilling his own oxygen tank Caspian found the others munching on protein bars, waiting for the adult's signal to head back out. Silently he bolstered their nerves with direct eye contact and a strong nod. *We can do this*, he wanted to communicate. *We will be the ones to end this, on our terms.*

Once the humans reentered the water, the sea snakes replaced the jellyfish, relieving them of their shark guard duty. The jellyfish would take longer to travel away, and the snake's poison was just as strong a deterrent as the jellyfish's tentacles. The mixture of the pink illuminated jellyfish skin and the orange remedy almost glowed against the night black water. As the scientists sprayed them, they quietly thanked the jellyfish for saving them time and again. Baptized back into the natural world, they floated off. Flynn was grateful they would stick together, that at they at least would still have each other, much like she and her siblings and friends would remain together as well. She smiled at that thought. Who would have thought that leaving the ARK and living on the surface for three months would bring her closer to the people she had intentionally left behind? Luke's gentle nudge to her shoulder brought her out of her thoughts and reminded her it was almost time to follow through with their plan.

The sharks were moving forward toward the humans, getting ready for their turn to transform. The sea snakes would momentarily hide in the cave with the children, providing a protective barrier between them and the sharks. The adults were armed with equal amounts of antidote and harpoons to protect themselves against the snapping teeth of the converted sharks. The subs moved in as well, ready to fire tranquilizer darts in case things got out of hand.

As soon as the adults had administered the antidote

they would rush to the sub, leaving the children to change the sea snakes and board in the same fashion as their parents. Flynn ducked into the cave behind Luke and grabbed his outstretched hand as they swam into the dark room.

"Hold steady," Caspian said, his voice reaching them through the ear piece imbeded into their SCUBA helmets. "Wait until the sharks begin to change and the adults' attention is fully occupied." Flynn, Luke, Pac, Stillman and Anton nodded their understanding. "Wait… hold it… ready… go."

The six friends turned away from the mouth of the cave and swam blindly into the cavern.

Chapter 64
Surface

"Light thinks it travels faster than anything but it is wrong. No matter how fast light travels, it finds the darkness has always got there first, and is waiting for it." – Terry Pratchett

"Are you sure your parents won't press charges for stealing their minivan?" Simon nervously asked for the hundredth time. Up until this point, he and the Nelson sisters had been discovering each other's past lives. Lives before they knew each other, lives that seemed infinitely more boring than the rollercoaster they had been living for the past few months. Their histories spilled from their mouths as the miles flew by the window.

"Like I said, I'll take the blame!" Nora said.

"Totally not believable," Simon argued. "You don't even have a license."

"Then I'll say I did it!" Nina said exasperatedly, and rolled her eyes for her sister's benefit. "Simon! This is your exit!"

Simon careened off the Florida State highway and followed the signs for the state park. A four lane road melted into two single lanes traveling in opposite directions. Eventually they left the asphalt behind and drove on a gravel road. The absence of street lights made Simon thankful for the full moon lighting their way.

When they pulled up to the state park entrance a dark windowed welcome cabin clearly communicated that the attendant was off duty. Rule follower by nature, Simon shoved twenty bucks inside one of the provided envelopes and dropped it in the collection box. He grabbed a park map, jumped back in the driver's seat and drove around the orange and white stripped blockade. Heading toward the coast, following the park signage they found a parking lot and put the car in park. Silently they grabbed their backpacks, removed their flashlights and got out of the van. After quickly checking their route on the map they walked to the trailhead and began the last leg of their journey on foot.

    The rush and crush of the ocean grew louder and louder the nearer they got to the shore. Careful not to step into any sink holes, they precariously hopped their way to the pinpointed marker on their map. Chirping cicadas and other surface night noises filled the air, but they weren't loud enough to cover the laundry list of worries that ran through their minds. What if they went to the wrong location? What if Caspian and the others got lost? Hurt? Killed?

    Suddenly Nina stopped, pulling them out of their internal monologues of fear and back to the present moment.

    "I think this is it," Nina said, her eyes drifting from the map, to the landscape around her and back to the map again. Nora consulted the GPS on her phone and made the same conclusion. The trio toed just a bit further before reaching the edge of an opening in the ground. They dropped to their knees and pulled the overgrowth of brush away to fully reveal the prized location of their nocturnal scavenger hunt. They'd found the land entry point to Adonis' sea cave lair.

    "All right little buddy," Simon cooed as he pulled the fish-cam from his backpack. "Time to go to work." Simon flipped all of the appropriated switches and then gently placed the fish in the water. The moon's reflection on the surface of the water made it hard to see the fish-cam as Simon maneuvered it down into the cave, but within a minute, Nora had pulled up the newly installed video feed app and together they huddled around the glowing screen of her phone to both navigate and follow its progress. Still, the dark water surrounding the fish didn't allow them much of a view until Simon tapped a button on his control, and light filled the space of the cave.

"Late night addition," Simon said, sheepishly awash in looks of amazement.

Now that they could properly see, Nina consulted the sea cave map Caspian had given her and dictated for Simon the route he should travel. Expertly and efficiently he wound his way through the cave, looking for either Caspian and the crew, or the giant squid that called herself Nycho.

"It's hard to believe this is real," Simon said, moving his thumbs at lightning speed. "I feel like I'm playing a video game."

"Science can be pretty cool huh?" Nina asked with a wide smile.

"Totally," Simon answered mirroring her smile.

"Before you two completely geek out," Nora said mockingly. "I think we better pay attention to whatever that thing is coming into view right now."

Chapter 65
Underwater Cave

"An idea is salvation by imagination." – Frank Lloyd Wright

Barely a hundred yards into the cave, they encountered their first wild life.

"How's it feel to be rebels?" Jett asked swimming forward to greet his friends.

"I think you should be asking yourself that question," Pac said with a grin. "We have our parents to answer to, which is bad enough, but I'm sure Mother Nature is probably pretty pissed right about now too. And that's your problem."

"Probably," Jett agreed. "But I'll deal with it when I have too."

"Nice plan Luke," 'Cuda complimented. "The adults didn't even notice when we snuck away into the cave."

"Thanks, let's just say the art of distraction is a skill I come by honestly. I've practiced it to perfection. It's not our fault the grownups can't keep track of hundreds of moving creatures at the same time. There were bound to be a few escapees."

"Speaking of," Caspian cut in. "Have you seen anyone else around?"

"No, we are the only onesssss."

"Pelamis!" Caspian said in plain shock. "I wasn't sure you'd join us."

"I wasssn't sssure myssself until the lassst moment. But here I am."

"Glad you have," Caspian said seriously to which Pelamis nodded silently. Caspian looked around the cavern, taking stock of the creatures that surrounded him. Jett, 'Cuda, Pelamis, Kurma, and Hale all floated before him. After a closer inspection he could see Aster clinging to Kurma's shell, along for whatever may come their way. They had all come and appeared unaffected by the antidote that permeated the water outside the cave.

"Alright," said Luke taking command. "Phase two."

Time was of the essence and they wasted none of it. Caspian quickly briefed everyone on their next steps and in a matter of minutes they were off and swimming. Caspian and Anton led the way with Luke directly behind, harpoon in tow. Jett brought up the rear, protecting them from the backside, and keeping his tentacles clear of the human's flipper clad appendages. The rest of the crew lay in between and above, swimming quickly, but cautiously.

"Stop!" Caspian said throwing his hand up like a crossing guard. "Do you hear that?"

"It's freaky enough in here without you being all dramatic," Flynn voiced her annoyance.

"He's right! Shh, listen," 'Cuda said.

Amid the bubbles and gurgles of their SCUBA tanks another distinctive sound could be heard. Like fingernails tapping on a table. Hundreds and hundreds of them. At the front of the group Caspian and Anton prepared to douse the incoming animals with antidote if necessary.

Luke leveled the harpoon between the space that separated Caspian and Anton. The rest of the group hung back, positioning themselves up against the walls of the cave, out of the way. The sound grew louder and closer. It was no longer necessary to strain their ears to hear the sound of claws scrabbling across the cave floor. In the blink of an eye the dark passageway went from empty to overflowing with the forms of hundreds of Blue Beauty Crabs.

"Everybody up!" Caspian instructed. The kids and animals bolted to the ceiling of the cavern, narrowly avoiding the thousands of hazardous pincers.

"They aren't talking," Stillman observed, "Only trying

to get out of the cave. They must not be changed." They watched the tide of crabs rush from the cave and wondered what fueled their speedy departure... hunger or fear. As the last of the crabs retreated and the crew's heartbeats slowed, they sank back to the floor of the cave.

"Well, shall we proceed?" Caspian's question was met with silence and head bobs of approval. Nervously they swam forward determined to complete their mission.

They continued through the labyrinth. When reaching a fork in their path, they always traveled north and west, further into the coastal lands of Florida. They left no breadcrumbs behind them, confident their subsea compass would lead them out of the maze if they needed to exit the same way they entered.

In truth, they planned to exit through a cave opening in the ceiling onto land. Their lives depended on that plan working. Who knew how long it would take to find, subdue and transform Nycho? What they did know was that they had an hour and a half left of oxygen in their tanks, so they better not delay. As one turn led to another underwater corridor, led to another great room, led to another passageway, Flynn tried to quiet the nagging voice in her head that sounded remarkably like her mother, reminding her just how dangerous sea caves were and exactly how many divers died in them each year. If they were going to consider this mission a success, they would all need to be alive and breathing after they accomplished their task.

In order to do that, they could waste no time. Against her rising panic about their time schedule Flynn was just about to suggest they paused to consult the cave map when a rumbling voice echoed through the tunneled hallways. Their forward movement instantly froze while their heads spun around wildly searching for the source of the voice.

"You're getting close little land walkers. It's not far now."

When the group looked questioningly at Caspian he responded,

"Well, we didn't come all this way to swim back with our proverbial tails between our legs."

"Amen," Luke said hoisting the harpoon again.

Swimming a bit slower now, the group edged around every corner, bracing themselves for the sight that would send shivers of fear down their spines. North, north, west, north... they continued to swim, taking the turns as their compass guided them farther and farther inland. As they approached the next corner a small streamlined form came buzzing straight at them, causing them all to gasp and most of them to curse.

"Holy sea silt that scared me," Stillman said.

"Sorry," the little fish responded.

"Simon?" Flynn asked.

"Yep!" Simon replied. "And Nora! And Nina!" they could hear the girls shout in the background.

"Oh thank Poseidon," Caspian said. "Do you know the way out?"

"Yes, it's about a quarter mile east from where you are right now. And the beast is just in there. Watch out, she's hungry. I almost didn't get away," Simon warned.

"What do you mean she's still in there? She didn't come after you?" Flynn asked.

"Only with her tentacles. For some reason, she's refusing to leave the cave."

"Interesting," Stillman said, appearing deep in thought.

"I'm still sticking with psycho," Flynn mumbled.

"Alright," Caspian said taking charge again. "We're going in. You wait out here Simon, ready to show us our escape route. We're still pretty good on oxygen, and close enough to the surface to not have to worry too much about oxygen bubbles in our blood from a quick surfacing. Just be ready to help haul us out as fast as possible."

"Got it," Simon said and Caspian was confident that he did.

Chapter 66
Surface

"It felt like forever. He would be patient, because he had no choice."
From: Jefferson's Sons by Kimberly Brubaker Bradly

Nina paced around the cave opening, wearing a path through the grasses and sea oats. She tried to ignore the constant buzzing of her phone created by the multiple incoming calls and text messages from her parents.

"Maybe I should tell them something," Nina worried. "Like we went to a movie, or we're at the PitStop."

"Those are too easy to check out and when they find out we are not there, we will get into more trouble for lying," Nora said, her eyes fixed on the pool of water before her. "Flynn and the others have be coming soon. Once they are out, we can text them we're okay and on our way."

"For the love of Poseidon, on our way from where?" Nina persisted.

"I don't know little mermaid, we'll make something up, but just give it a rest," Nora hissed. "And quit with all the underwater mumbo jumbo already."

"I'm just trying to –"

"Enough!" Simon shouted silencing the girls. It was the first time they had ever heard him yell. His cheeks turned red enough to see in the moonlight and Nora was willing to bet that the tips of his ears, tucked under his favorite stocking cap, were burning as well. An awkward silence hung between the three of them for a bit before Simon said, "I know you guys could get in a lot of trouble with your parents, but did you ever think about me? I could get expelled for something like this."

"Right," Nora started by way of apology. "Sorry."

"Me too," Nina said. A few minutes passed in silence while Simon repeatedly wiped his sweaty hands on his pants, Nora stared at the pool of water and Nina eyed up the country bright constellations in the sky.

"Is there anything we can do to help them?" Nina asked quietly.

"I don't think so. The only thing we can do right now, is wait," Simon said regretfully.

Chapter 67
Underwater Cave

"He had read lots of stories where heroes succeeded in spite of long odds, where they accomplished a task that everyone else had failed at. He wondered for the first time about all the people who'd gone before those heroes, about whether they'd been heroic too, or whether they'd been at each other's throats, before everything had gone wrong. He wondered if there was a point where they realized they weren't going to make it, weren't going to beat the long odds – that in the legend that would follow, they were going to be the nameless people that failed." – from: Dollbones by Holly Black

Simon had been right. Nycho was not leaving the cave. In fact she was not even leaving the corner of the cave in which she huddled. Caspian and the crew were able to swim into the expansive room and float just out of her reach in remarkable safety.

"So, we meet at last. You may call me Nycho, Queen of the Ocean," the giant squid said introducing herself. She was not far off. Her size alone, demanded respect and reverence. It was easy to see why she had so systematically claimed the obedience of all she had encountered. Her head alone was over ten feet tall, finishing in a stately point that wouldn't be hard to imagine as the resting place for a crown. Her cloudy eyes were the size of beach balls. Black and colorless, they seemed to float on an otherwise featureless face. From this center form stretched eight tentacles armored with razor sharp suction cups, hungry to slice its prey to ribbons before ingesting it through the unseen mouth that lay waiting on its underside.

"What is it you want? And why should we give it to you?" Caspian asked, attempting to play the role of a diplomat.

"The world we live in is no longer safe. You land walkers have destroyed it with your garbage and chemicals and pollution. How are we to live in this toxic fish bowl you have created for us? How are we to survive? Who will pay for the mistakes you have made?"

"That's a lovely little rant, but you still haven't answered our question," Flynn snapped back.

"What do I want?" Nycho asked bitterly. "I want revenge."

"Then take it!" Luke shouted losing his cool. "Here we are! Make us pay!" Flynn pulled his arm back, away from the trigger of the harpoon. They only had one shot. It would not be good to waste it on an uncalculated move of anger.

"You?" Nycho laughed fiendishly. "Your lives? Who do you think you are? Your lives do not add up in the balance of all the damage your kind has done. Your lives would not even begin to pay the land walkers debt. No, no. I have other plans, better plans, bigger plans." At this she swam away from the corner, causing everyone to jump backward. But she did not attack. Instead she revealed row upon row of swaying seaweed, a veritable farmland of the green crop. Nestled at the base of each frond were dozens and dozens of eggs. Nycho's eggs.

Devastating realization hit them all in the same moment. She was growing an army. One bigger and more deadly than a thousand Water Warriors. This was her plan. This was why she refused to leave. Adonis was right. He was only a distraction. She needed time. And loyal to the end, he gave her that. But the question now was, how much more time did she need? When would the eggs hatch? And would they talk? Would they think?

"I can see the questions racing through your brain," Nycho said apparently amused. "It is almost time. And when they hatch I know they will be like me, like you. I talk to them even now and I hear their responses. They speak to their mother already. When my darlings are born they will talk and they will think and I will raise them to hate you. And then, we will end you."

As she talked Caspian noticed a disturbance in the sand along the floor of the cave. A thin line traveled closer to the rows of sea weed and then disappeared into the vegetation. When he raised his arm to point it out Anton casually pushed it back down to his side. With a peripheral glance and a tiny shake of his head, he told Caspian to remain quiet.

Nycho ranted on. Disease, pollution, garbage. Revenge, hate, an unstoppable army. Her babies, her warriors, her assassins. The people of the world would know her wrath and then they would die at the tentacles of her offspring. She turned from the humans to her eggs and back again, using her tentacles to gesticulate her passion. All the while the humans stood before her motionless and listened.

Caspian felt foolish that he was the only one who had needed to be told not to point out their animal friend's movement. And even if he could not see Pelamis now, he knew what he was doing. Bite by bite, ounce by poisonous ounce, he was killing the eggs. The longer Nycho continued to rant, the more he would have time to kill. If only he had brought more sea snakes with him.

"For weeks now I have been stuck in this cave, leaving only for short bursts of time. I have been starving without company. Not even that fool Adonis comes to visit me anymore."

"That's because he's dead," Luke said. "And Marianus too."

"The rest have been returned to their natural form," Caspian explained, praying to Poseidon she would ask them how. And she did. In a halting way, Caspian explained the long process, stalling as much as possible.

"Well aren't you clever. But not clever enough to stop

me. And unfortunately now that you know my plans, I cannot allow you to leave. Plus, I am hungry. Any volunteers?" she asked, her tentacles raising from the floor, poised for attack. "No? Oh well, beggars can't be choosers, I've always liked a challenge anyway." Rising up to her full measure and spreading her tentacles out she made the enormous cave feel crowded.

Flynn, Stillman, Pac and the rest of their animal friends began to slowly edge backward, giving the others plenty of room. No matter how badly 'Cuda wanted to sink his razor sharp teeth into Nycho and Jett wanted to sting her, they could not be present for the next phase of the plan. Still Nycho's tentacles spilled outward, extending their reach. Just as she was about to attack Pelamis made his presence known behind her.

"Sssquid, before you kill these human friends of mine, can you answer just one question?"

"What? Who? Where did you come from?" Nycho sputtered.

"You do have another nessst of eggs available for your hossstile takeover correct? Becaussse I think you'll find thessse onesss a little... how ssshould I put thisss? Dead."

"Nooooooooo!" Nycho's scream filled the cave. As her tentacles simultaneously reached out for Pelamis he dove deep into Nycho's nest of grasses.

"Now!" Caspian yelled turning Nycho's attention again to her human meal. Luke launched the harpoon straight at one of the monster's giant eyes. The bladed shaft sailed through the water with deadly speed. With incredible accuracy it hit Nycho in the center of her pupil and again the cave was filled with her screams. As everyone else swam away to safety Caspian and Anton and Pac unleashed steady streams of the antidote from their squirt guns, changing the water from transparent to a milky orange.

The confusion of the change and the pain of the

harpoon completely overwhelmed and occupied the giant squid. Her tentacles thrashed violently but without specific direction and purpose. The three boys back stroked out of the cave, continuing to dispense the antidote as they exited the cave. Not wishing to be encumbered by their burden a second longer they dropped their packs the second they were outside the cave and sprinted to catch up with the rest of the crew.

Nycho's verbal assault turned to an inhuman scream. Fear fueled their burst of speed. Following the light of Simon's fish-cam, the trio found their way to the land entrance. They reached the ceiling opening of the cave just as Stillman's flipper left the water. Caspian pushed Anton to the surface where he was hauled from the water by shaking hands. Then he pulled Pac from behind him to exit next. His head swiveled a new direction every second, searching for the tentacles he was sure would squeeze the life out of him. When the firm grip around his biceps finally grabbed him, he let out an involuntary shriek and thrashed from side to side.

It took him several seconds to realize that it was Nina who smothered him, hugging his soaking form with a power that would rival even Nycho's tentacles.

Three weeks later

Chapter 68
Surface

"Go with the punches and take the hits. Sometimes I mess up, I eff up, I swing and miss. But it's okay, I'm cool with this. I still fall on my face sometimes and I can't color inside the lines. 'Cause I'm perfectly incomplete. I'm still working on my masterpiece." – from: Masterpiece by Jessie J

Nora found the crew, in her room, sprawled on the bed and floor completely absorbed in the collection yearbooks she had amassed in her sixteen years. She smiled down at them all benevolently. Flynn lay on her belly next to Luke, both smiling, legs and feet entwined. Nina was of course next to Caspian, explaining every detail of last year's edition, proudly pointing out each and every nerdy club photo in which she appeared. Pac and Anton were checking out the cheerleaders while Noah was eyeing up the sports section. Stillman and Sonora each had their noses buried too, their geeky fascination with learning still apparent, even on the surface.

"So," Nora started drawing attention to her presence. "After school I bust my butt at soccer practice all afternoon while the rest of you just laze around all day? Is this how life is gonna be now that you are living on the surface full time?"

"To be fair," Stillman piped up. "We missed out on tryouts. We did only officially start surface school last week."

"And… technically, I think sports would register as fun," Pac pointed out "And we're all still definitely grounded for another month… or six." His remark was met by half-hearted laughter.

"Thanks for the reminder!" Luke said hurling a pillow at his head.

"Hey! Easy!" Nora shouted as she picked her way

across the room to her closet. "Flynn, we're leaving in 20 minutes."

"Where are we going?" Flynn asked

"Your driver's test," Nora answered.

"My what?" Flynn shrieked.

"Well, technically it's my driver's test, but I'm giving my time slot to you. I figured I still had a bit left in the owing column after well… you know. Ancient history, but whatever. Go on, get ready. I'm gonna shower and then we're out."

Flynn squealed her happiness, smothered Nora in a hug and then bolted from the room to get ready to go.

"Surface girls, all kinds of crazy," Pac said with an eye roll.

"Totally," Nora agreed. "I'll have the newly licensed driver bring me to the PitStop afterward if you all want to meet there in an hour." Nods and murmurs of approval followed her out the door which she shut behind her. Leaning back against it she closed her eyes, sighed and wished that life could remain like this forever.

Chapter 69
Outlier Station

"Friendship is the only cement that will ever hold the world together." – Woodrow Wilson

Caspian fidgeted in the submarine, itching with anticipation to arrive at the Outlier Station. Flynn looked across the aisle from where she sat and giggled at him.

"You look just like I did when I first went up to the surface."

"It's true," their father said, fully healed and at the helm of the sleek submarine. Caspian shrugged sheepishly and strained to see out the window again, looking for the beginning signs of the Outlier Station to come into view. As always, the docking and pressurizing seemed like the longest step. When they were finally safely attached to the station he rocketed out of his seat past the doorway, through the loading dock and to the wide expanse of the open window view from the living room.

It looked different since the last time they had been here. Other scientists, unconnected to the PE-328 catastrophe, had come and cleaned it up. They restocked the supplies and reset all of the facilities to fully functioning levels. Even the blankets were nicely folded and Savannah's fingerprints were wiped from the window's surface. But he wasn't looking at any of those things. His eyes frantically scanned the waters outside the station, searching for the silver scales of a friend.

"He's just gotta be here," Caspian whispered. "He has to." Flynn came up to stand behind him and put her hand on his shoulder.

"He can't be here all the time," she said softly so only he could hear.

Flynn and her parents and even Noah moved around the Outlier Station, performing their usual tasks and rituals. Mrs. Brinestone checked in on an experiment in the mini lab and Mr. Brinestone tested water samples for levels of pollution and any antidote remaining in the water. Noah filled the fish feeder and snapped pictures of the animals that came to graze on the fresh food. Flynn sat in the tech station, scrolling through the data that had been automatically collected in their absence. Caspian sat at the window. Watching. Waiting. His parents looked on with casual concern, but left him to his solitary position. Stress from a traumatic incident affected everyone differently and if this was how he needed to deal with it, they were willing to give him time and space.

The morning came and went quickly. Caspian refused to join them for lunch. The afternoon was filled with more chores and station maintenance for everyone else, but Caspian remained at the window. By late afternoon his stoic form had slumped against the window and his forehead rested against the glass. Even though it had been three month since he had be underwater, he knew it would be last light in a matter of minutes. Still he searched, his brain begging his eyes to see a form that wasn't really there.

But then, not so suddenly, Caspian's gaze was not languid. It began to have a focus. He could not pinpoint the moment he realized something had changed, but there was something definitely different about the scene. There was an object coming towards him. It wove back and forth, back and forth. Definitely not human. Not man-made either. It came closer and closer. Because of the station's sea level and the waning light, it was more of a moving shadow than a specific thing. Caspian began to stand up. He pressed his body against the glass like a two year old at the aquarium. And then, his face split open into a wide smile.

"I'm going out for a swim!" he shouted, racing for the

loading dock and clumsily pulling on his wet suit and fins.

"Dinner's in thirty minutes!" his father called, to which his mother replied,

"Take all the time you need Cas!" and his father nodded in agreement.

Caspian dove into the water and darted to the windowless back of the station. Rounding the corner he swam smack into the figure he had spent the day searching for. The two collided in a warm and friendly embrace.

"I worried you'd never come back," 'Cuda said into Caspian's armpit.

"I've been grounded for a long time. We all have. This is our first trip back," Caspian said releasing the barracuda. "I'll spare you the details, but let's just my mother's reaction to our little adventure made Nycho look like a toddler throwing a temper tantrum."

"Well, it's good to see you now, in one piece," 'Cuda said.

"It sure is. Been swimming safe?"

"And strong."

The two friends talked long past Caspian's thirty minute dinner time. 'Cuda told him of their escape from the cave. Blind in one eye, Nycho could not track them accurately and together the animal friends had made their way out of the cave. They agreed to patrol the cave exit in shifts until Nycho did finally emerge several hours later. She then retreated to the bottom of a deep ravine in the continental break and no one has seen or heard from her since.

"We will continue to watch her. I'll let you know if any trouble rises up again." Caspian nodded and then asked after the rest of the animals. Jett was still loving life. He didn't live with his parents anymore, but visited their colony of jellyfish often. He would rather explore the ocean than stay cooped up in one place, but when he visited his parents, he also stopped by the outlier station to see 'Cuda as well. The stories he had to tell were filled with adventure and 'Cuda assured Caspian the jellyfish was truly happy. Aster and Kurma continued to stick together, traveling the currents back and forth. Hale lived with his school of angelfish, but came by the station almost every evening to talk with 'Cuda. He was a good friend and 'Cuda was glad to have him.

"What about Pelamis?" Caspian asked tentatively.

"Pelamis made it out of the cave alive. After Nycho left and I tailed her, Jett remained at the cave watching and waiting for him to come out. He did, but changed. He can no longer speak the way we do. I check up on him from time to time, swimming as close to the League of Dark Vines as I dare. Now that most of us are back in our natural state, it's somewhat dangerous. But from what I've seen, he's with his family, his kind, and he is happy."

"I almost think it is better that way," Caspian said.

"I agree. I think this is what would make him most happy. Now, tell me about the surface. What adventures are you having there?" 'Cuda asked with interest.

Caspian told him all about the surface school. It was different, but good. Everyone was adjusting nicely. Flynn had gotten her driver's license and was happily dating Luke. Pac was a cheerleader magnet and loving the surf and sun. Anton and Stillman had teamed up to make a formidable addition to every nerdy club the school offered while Sonora and Nina decided to try out for the spring play. Nora swore off boys and decided to focus solely on soccer. Simon was crushed by this news, but rededicated his efforts to Professor Sorenson. Caspian was sure he was the next brilliant scientist of their time. Noah was a ten year old boy in heaven experiencing the surface's many wonders including Disney World, boogie boarding and skate parks. Everyone was happy and best of all, everyone was together again.

"What about the ARK?" 'Cuda asked.

"It's in shambles. And is probably going to stay that

way for a long time. Professor Sorenson has already started a fundraising campaign, but it will take years before there is enough money to fix it. For now, we are all taking turns coming to the Outlier Station. There will be someone here almost twenty four hours a day. We are signed up to come in two day rotations, but because of school, the kids can only come on the weekends. But I guess it's better than nothing. Maybe next Fall when Nina and I sign up for our classes at Bay City University we can schedule ourselves a three day weekend and get down here more often."

"Maybe one day, by the time you two have children, the ARK will be ready to live in again," 'Cuda said hopefully. Caspian rolled his eyes, but then smiled. "I should be going," 'Cuda said "the sharks come out about this time of night and I'd rather eat a meal than be one. But I think Jett is stopping by tomorrow, and Hale will come too. Meet me here again tomorrow night?"

"Absolutely. We're staying until Sunday evening so we've got some time to catch up," Caspian said. "Swim safe."

"Swim strong."

The two friends swam away to their respective sleeping places for the evening. The world had changed in a thousand ways since they had first met and Caspian was sure it would change a thousand times again in the years to come.
But the one thing that wouldn't change was the bond of friendship. They knew that no matter what happened in this crazy world that they could count on each other to show up for the wild ride.

Cast of Characters

ARK Crew

Brinestone Family: Dr. Arthur Brinestone, Mrs. Bermuda Brinestone, Caspian, Flynn and Noah

Stein Family: Mr. and Mrs. Stein, Stillman, Sonora

Conrad Family: Mr. and Mrs. Conrad, Luke

Peterson Family: Mr. Burke, Pacific (Pac)

Perone Family: Mr. and Mrs. Perone, Anton

Grier Family: Mr. and Mrs. Grier, Carl

Professor Bebee Johnston

Surface Characters

Nelson Family: Mr. and Mrs. Nelson, Nina, Nora

Professor Solomon Sorenson

Simon Ludkin

Savannah Taylor

Alex Christian

Kelsey Martin

Riley Hanson

ARK Allies

'Cuda (barracuda)

Steve, Adriel and Jett (jellyfish)

Pelamis (sea snake)

Hale (angelfish)

Kurma (sea turtle)

Aster (starfish)

Water Warriors

Adonis (dolphin)

Marianus (Mahi)

Dathan (swordfish)

Nycho (giant squid)

Other Minor Characters

Silas (barracuda guard)

Mrs. Worthington (Professor Sorenson's secretary)

Darla and Dallas (news anchors)

Author's Note

This book would not have been possible if it weren't for the flexibility, grace and understanding of my husband Matt. Thank you for allowing me the time in our crazy busy lives to pursue my dreams.

To my sister Kate, who told me: "Don't just end it because you are tired of writing, I hate when authors do that". This advice helped me focus in on the best possible ending I could write, thank you. Thank you to my beta-readers, advice givers, email readers and cover selectors... Sarah, Becky, Andrew, Manuela, Kate, Terry and Matt, I appreciate your endless support and encouragement. To the Brookman's, my favor granting fairies, thank you for resurrecting my computer, checking my every comma and for being darned good friends.

As always I have my celebrity inspirations, those written word confidants who lead me through their shining exemplars of enchanting work. Thank you Margaret Peterson Haddix, Holly Black, Ben Mikaelsen, Polly Holyoke, Gordon Korman and countless others who fill my middle school teaching days with pure reading pleasure. Thank you also to lyrical genius Taylor Swift, for being a role model extraordinaire for artists and females everywhere.

And finally, thank you reader's for joining me on this journey. I hope you'll follow me on more to come.

Happy reading,
Amanda Zieba

Author's Bio

Amanda Zieba is a full time reading teacher, a mother and wife always and a writer any minute she can squeeze in. This is her fifth book and has plans for many, many more. She lives in the great state of Wisconsin with her husband and two sons. When she is not reading or writing you can find her eating poptarts, getting her nails done, going on walks or building the most amazing Lego creations known to man with her sons.

Previous Books by Amanda Zieba

Breaking the Surface

Charles Christmas Gift

Joanna's Journey

Irish Strong William

Amanda can be found online on her Facebook page:
Amanda Zieba - Author